PARIS MATCH

BOOKS BY STUART WOODS

FICTION

Cut and Thrust[†]

Carnal Curiosity[†]

Standup Guy[†]

Doing Hard Time[†]

Unintended Consequences[†]

Collateral Damage[†]

Severe Clear[†]

Unnatural Acts[†]

DC Dead[†]

Son of Stone[†]

Bel-Air Dead[†]

Strategic Moves[†]

Santa Fe Edge[§]

Lucid Intervals[†]

Kisser[†]

Hothouse Orchid[*]

Loitering with Intent[†]

Mounting Fears[‡]

Hot Mahogany[†]

Santa Fe Dead[§]

Beverly Hills Dead

Shoot Him If He Runs[†]

Fresh Disasters[†]

Short Straw[§]

Dark Harbor[†]

Iron Orchid[*]

Two-Dollar Bill[†]

The Prince of Beverly Hills

Reckless Abandon[†]

Capital Crimes[‡]

Dirty Work[†]

Blood Orchid[*]

The Short Forever[†]

Orchid Blues[*]

Cold Paradise[†]

L.A. Dead[†]

The Run[‡]

Worst Fears Realized[†]

Orchid Beach[*]

Swimming to Catalina[†]

Dead in the Water[†]

Dirt[†]

Choke

Imperfect Strangers

Heat

Dead Eyes

L.A. Times

Santa Fe Rules[§]

New York Dead[†]

Palindrome

Grass Roots[‡]

White Cargo

Deep Lie[‡]

Under the Lake

Run Before the Wind[‡]

Chiefs[‡]

TRAVEL

A Romantic's Guide to the Country Inns of Britain and Ireland (1979)

MEMOIR

Blue Water, Green Skipper

A Holly Barker Novel[*]

A Stone Barrington Novel[†]

A Will Lee Novel[‡]

An Ed Eagle Novel[§]

PARIS MATCH

STUART WOODS

G. P. PUTNAM'S SONS   *New York*

G. P. PUTNAM'S SONS
Publishers Since 1838
Published by the Penguin Group
Penguin Group (USA) LLC
375 Hudson Street,
New York, New York 10014

USA · Canada · UK · Ireland · Australia
New Zealand · India · South Africa · China

penguin.com
A Penguin Random House Company

Library of Congress Cataloging-in-Publication Data

Woods, Stuart.
Paris match / Stuart Woods.
p.   cm.—(Stone Barrington; 31)
ISBN 978-0-399-16912-0
1. Barrington, Stone (Fictitious character)—Fiction.   2. Private investigators—Fiction.
3. Paris (France)—Fiction.   I. Title.
PS3573.O642P37   2014   2014018596
813'.54—dc23

Printed in the United States of America
1   3   5   7   9   10   8   6   4   2

BOOK DESIGN BY NICOLE LAROCHE

PARIS
MATCH

S tone Barrington closed his three suitcases and called down for Fred Flicker to fetch his luggage. Fred was quick.

"I'll have the car around in five minutes, Mr. Barrington," he said.

"Thank you, Fred."

Fred hustled the three cases onto the elevator and disappeared. Stone turned to Ann Keaton, who was sitting on the end of his bed, fully dressed and ready to go to her job at the New York City campaign headquarters of Katharine Lee, the Democratic nominee for president of the United States. Ann was her deputy campaign manager.

"Are you crying because I'm leaving?" Stone asked. "I

mean, you've known for weeks that I have to go to Paris for the opening of the new hotel, l'Arrington."

"No," she said, "that's not why."

"I'll be back in two or three weeks, and you're going to be so busy with the campaign that you won't even notice that I'm gone."

"I'll notice," Ann said. "I have something to tell you."

"Just a minute," Stone said. He buzzed his secretary, Joan Robertson. "Ask Fred to pick up the Bacchettis, then come back for me," he said. Then he returned and sat next to Ann on the bed.

"All right," he said, "tell me."

"I'm crying because I won't be here when you get back," Ann said.

This was news to Stone. "And where will you be?"

"In Washington."

"I don't understand, Kate said you could work out of New York."

"Kate changed her mind," Ann said. "She wants me to work with Sam more closely. She wants us to meet every day, and Sam can't come to New York." Sam Meriwether, the senior senator from Georgia, was Kate Lee's campaign manager.

"And this is until the election?" Stone asked hopefully.

"Only if Kate isn't elected," Ann said. "We've talked about what happens if she gets elected: I'll be heading up the search operation for administration appointees, while remaining her chief of staff. And after the inauguration . . ."

"As the president's chief of staff, you'll be the second-most-powerful person in the world?"

"That's what everybody says," Ann said, then she renewed her crying.

"Ann, I can understand that if you have to choose between being with me and being the second-most-powerful person in the world, why you might not choose me."

"And I hate that about myself!" she sobbed. "Why do I want that above personal happiness?"

"Because you'd be doing it for your country," Stone said, "and, of course, because you'd be the second-most-powerful person in the world."

"Do you hate me?" Ann asked.

"Of course not. I love you."

"But you're not *in* love with me, not anymore."

"That's a self-defense mechanism," Stone said. "I know I can't have you, so I can't be in love."

"I can understand that," she said. "Everybody's got to protect himself. Still, I wish *you* were the one crying."

"I hardly ever cry," Stone said.

"You should try it sometime, it's good for you."

"I'll have to take your word for it." He got up, took her hand, and pulled her to her feet. "Come on, let's go down. I have to pick up my briefcase from Joan."

They took the elevator down to his office, where his briefcase stood open on his desk, with Joan standing guard.

"I got you ten thousand euros," she said. "If you need more, you can just use your ATM card. The bank says it works in Europe."

"I'll keep that in mind," Stone said. "But I don't see how I can spend ten thousand euros in two or three weeks."

"You'll find a way," Joan said, with a confidence born of keeping him in cash.

"Is the car out front?"

"Yes, everything's ready."

"Come on, I'll drop you at your office," he said to Ann.

"No," she said. "I want to walk, get some fresh air and get over feeling sorry for myself, and that will take a few minutes."

She walked him out to the car, where Fred already had the rear door open. He kissed Ann goodbye, got in, and kissed Viv Bacchetti on the cheek. Fred closed the door and got behind the wheel.

"Where's Dino?" he asked. Her husband, the newly minted commissioner of police for New York, was coming to Paris with them, where he was attending a conference of high-ranking police officials from Europe and the United States. They were taking the Gulfstream 650 jet belonging to Strategic Services, Viv's employer and the world's second-largest security company. She was to oversee the security staff at the new hotel, until things were running smoothly.

"He's coming in his car," she said, "or rather his motorcade. He had to pick up the L.A. chief of police and the Boston commissioner. The only way the mayor would let Dino ride in a corporate jet was if the other two guys came along, too, and

Mike Freeman was okay with that. It's a motorcade, because those guys are each traveling with two of their own detectives." Freeman was the CEO of Strategic Services.

"Okay, let's go, Fred."

"You look funny," Viv said.

"Funny queer or funny ha-ha?"

"Funny queer."

"I just had to say goodbye to Ann."

"Well, she'll be here when you get back."

"No, she'll be in Washington, very likely for years to come. Kate wants her there to work more closely with Sam Meriwether."

"I see."

"Yeah, so do I, but I don't like it much."

"Maybe it's not such a bad thing, Stone, maybe it's time for you to be a free man again."

Stone didn't know how to reply to that.

AT TETERBORO they were let through the security gate at Jet Aviation and Fred drove them to the big airplane. There was a line of black SUVs already there, disgorging men in suits and their luggage. Mike Freeman was greeting them at the airplane's door and turning them over to the two stewardesses, who would settle them in. Someone got their luggage out of the trunk, then Stone followed Viv up the stairs and to their seats. Dino made the introductions, then the three of them occupied seats together, along with Mike Freeman. The moment everyone was buckled into a seat, the airplane was taxiing. With no delay, they were on the runway, then down the runway and climbing.

"Paris awaits," Mike said.

"Are you looking forward to it?" Stone asked.

"I always do. By the way, Stone, you won't be driving into the city with us."

"Why not?"

"Because I had a call from Lance Cabot this morning." Cabot was the director of Central Intelligence. "His people will be transporting you."

"That's very weird," Stone said.

"I thought so, too," Mike replied.

And then they were eating a big breakfast.

S tone stepped out the door of the Gulfstream 650 and, from the top of the stairs, viewed what seemed a whole lot of badly parked SUVs. They were there to transport the occupants of the G-650 and their detectives, bodyguards, and the police officers who had come to greet them. One vehicle stood out: a white Mercedes van that was bigger and taller than the usual van. Leaning against it, grinning, was one Richard LaRose, known as Rick, who was the newly appointed Paris station chief of the Central Intelligence Agency. As Stone walked toward the man he caught sight of a Gulfstream 450 being towed into a nearby hangar, and he saw something familiar painted on an engine nacelle, a symbol he had seen before.

"Stone!" Rick yelled.

Stone turned and waved, then pointed out his luggage to a lineman, then pointed at the big van, then he strolled over and shook hands with the grinning Rick, forgetting the Gulfstream. "Rick, how are you?"

"Better than fine," Rick replied, "and I rate better transportation these days." He jerked a thumb toward the van. Rick's former transport had been a battered gray Ford van that he had done terrible things to.

"Congratulations on the new job," Stone said. "Lance mentioned it."

Stone's luggage was stored in a rear compartment, then Rick slid open the door of the van to reveal an interior that was more jetliner than van: four seats, two abreast, facing across a burled walnut tabletop. The cabin was swathed in soft beige leather. On one of the seats sat Lance Cabot, director of Central Intelligence, offering Stone a small, cool smile.

Stone got in and shook hands. "What a surprise to see you in Paris, Lance," he said. He always was wary around Lance, today no less so.

"In my line of work I try to surprise," Lance said. "When people expect you, bad things can happen."

Rick slid in beside Lance and closed the door, then rapped sharply on the bulkhead behind him. The van moved smoothly away

"What brings you across the pond?" Stone asked, genuinely curious.

Lance gazed out the window at the passing scenery. "Oh, I

thought I'd come over and help Rick get settled into his new office. And into his new job."

"And that is very much appreciated, Lance," Rick said, somehow avoiding sounding obsequious.

"Also, I wanted the opportunity to speak with you privately before you reach your new hotel," Lance said.

"Well, here I am, and this looks private to me. Assuming we can trust Rick, of course."

"Of course," Lance said. "Stone, your arrival in Paris coincides with two notable gatherings in the city: one is the meeting of that group of important policemen, now called the Congress of Security, or in the way of the world these days, CONSEC. Although many of these gentlemen have met at one time or another, this is the first time all of them have met at once. The importance of that meeting is indicated by the place of their conference, the Élysée Palace, which, as you know, is the seat of the president of France."

Stone nodded; he knew that much, at least.

"The other gathering, which will not be publicized, is of a criminal nature, though it will appear to be a conference of business executives. This is an organization of Russian oligarchs, most of them former KGB generals and colonels, who have grown rich and fat in their new, so-called democracy. What was formerly a loose network of old chums, colleagues, and enemies has now gelled into a more formal entity, which they call the Cowl, as in the hood of a monk. The apparent head monk is Yevgeny Majorov, the son of a very, very important KGB general, now thankfully deceased, and the brother of another decedent, Yuri Majorov, in whose death they suspect you of having had a hand."

Stone raised a finger. "I deny that," he said.

"Deny it all you like," Lance replied. "The fact is that Yuri wanted you dead because you would not accept him as a partner in your hotel business, and he had brought with him to Los Angeles a feared mafia assassin, who sometimes worked freelance, for the express purpose of ensuring your demise."

"I believe I heard something about that," Stone said.

"Yuri, as we now know, departed Los Angeles in his private jet, bound for Moscow, and arrived in that city, having apparently expired of natural causes en route."

Stone shrugged. "These things happen."

"Yuri's death coincided with that of his hired assassin, in his bed at the Bel-Air Hotel, and his killer used a little something from the gentleman's own pharmaceutical supply to off both the assassin and Yuri."

"There's a certain poetry to that," Stone observed.

"Yes, and that standard of 'poetry' is rarely found outside organizations such as the one I head. In fact, I believe this particular 'poet' to be a former member of my flock, one Teddy Fay, but I can't prove it, and that fact alone causes me to suspect Teddy. That and the fact that Teddy's name, photographs, fingerprints, and DNA test have recently vanished from every intelligence and law enforcement database in the United States and its possessions, along with the databases of all those nations with whom we share such data."

"I will have to take the Fifth on that one," Stone said.

"There is only one way this could have happened," Lance said. "Not even I could have engineered it, and I can engineer almost anything, if I try hard enough. No, that action originated far, far above my pay grade. One, and only one, personage could have initiated it, and he, coincidentally, is a friend of yours. But, for reasons of both decorum and self-preservation, I will say no more about that."

"Thank you, Lance, that is a relief."

"Good, but you have little else about which to be relieved, Stone."

"What is that supposed to mean?"

"It means that Yevgeny Majorov has made some of the same deductions I have made, and he believes you, in one way or another, to be responsible for both his brother's failure to penetrate the ownership of your hotel group and for his brother's untimely demise."

"The man must be delusional," Stone said.

"Nevertheless," Lance said, "while you are in Paris you are going to have to watch your ass—or rather, Rick and his coterie are going to have to. Do you understand and accept this fact?"

Stone sighed. "If I must," he said.

"Yes, you must. Good day to you." The van glided to a stop at a Paris street corner; Lance exited the vehicle and immediately got into a black sedan.

"Now to l'Arrington," Rick said.

ick's van took so many turns down so many narrow streets that Stone lost his bearings. After a time, however, the van slowed for a left turn, and Stone saw, for the first time, the gates to the new hotel. They turned and drove through a handsome archway into a large courtyard. A building that was probably impressive under ordinary circumstances had been concealed by acres of scaffolding and plastic cloth.

"I believe they're sandblasting the limestone facade," Rick said.

"I hope the inside looks better," Stone said.

"What was this place before it was a hotel?" Rick asked.

"It was a hotel," Stone replied. "Before that it was a hospital that Marcel duBois's father had bought and turned into a cheap hotel. Marcel has now turned it into an expensive one."

Stone alit from the big van and discovered that it had been followed by three black SUVs, which now disgorged Dino and Viv Bacchetti, Mike Freeman, and the top policemen of Los Angeles and Boston and their luggage.

Dino came over and peeked into Rick's van. "I want one of these," he said.

Stone introduced everybody to Rick, while a team of bellmen erupted from the hotel to collect all their luggage.

"Is this place finished?" Dino asked, looking around.

"Almost," Stone said. "The paint in your room may still be wet, though."

There was no check-in process; they were immediately escorted into elevators, and Stone was shown into a large, elegantly furnished suite, while Dino and Viv were put in an adjoining bedroom.

A large crystal vase of calla lilies stood on a table in Stone's living room, and he read the attached card. *Welcome to your new home in Paris*, it said, and was signed by Marcel duBois.

Dino and Viv unpacked and returned to the sitting room, where tea and some light food had been brought up.

"When do we see Marcel duBois?" Viv asked.

"You'll see him at dinner. Dino, when do your meetings start?"

"The day after tomorrow. We're supposed to get over the jet

lag during that time. What was the deal with the white van?" Dino asked.

"It contained Lance Cabot," Stone explained, "who wanted to tell me that the Russians haven't forgotten about me."

"Oh, shit," Dino said.

"Am I going to have to provide your security?" Viv asked.

"No, Lance has thoughtfully taken care of that. Rick LaRose, who you just met, is the CIA's Paris station chief, newly in the job."

"What's Lance doing in Paris?" Dino asked.

"He says he came to help Rick settle into his new office, but I tend to think that nothing Lance says is ever entirely true."

"How long do we have until dinner?" Viv asked.

Stone looked at his watch. "An hour."

"Then please excuse me, I have a lot to do." She vanished into their room.

"Me, too," Dino said. "See you later." He followed Viv.

Stone went to do his own unpacking and freshening.

THE WHITE Mercedes van awaited them in the courtyard, *sans* Rick.

"Where are we going?" Dino asked.

"To a wonderful restaurant called Lasserre," Stone said. "Marcel duBois is our host, and I understand there will be some other people there, too."

They arrived at the restaurant, in the Avenue Franklin Roosevelt, and were taken up in an elevator. They walked into a large, square dining room with a sunken center. To Stone's surprise, all the guests were milling around the room, drinking champagne and talking with each other.

Marcel duBois broke from a knot of people and came across the room, arms spread. There followed the usual kissing of both cheeks, and Stone reintroduced him to Dino and Viv. "Marcel," he said, "why is no one dining?"

"Because I have not yet told them to," Marcel replied.

"Do you mean you've taken the whole restaurant?"

"I had to. I couldn't get everyone I wanted you to meet into my dining room at home."

"Who are these people?"

"The *crème de la crème* of Paris, of course," Marcel replied. "Business, show business, hotel business, writing business, you name it. Come and meet them."

For half an hour they were ushered from group to group and introduced. When they were done, Stone could remember only one name: Mirabelle Chance, who was about five-two barefoot, raven of hair and ivory of complexion.

"Come, let us sit down," Marcel said.

At a signal from Marcel a chime rang, and the guests began finding their place cards. Marcel headed the table in the very center of the room.

Viv looked up. "The roof is opening," she said. She was right: the frescoed ceiling slid open to reveal a rose arbor on the roof.

"Whenever it gets a bit too warm," Marcel explained, "the ceiling opens and lets out the hot air."

Stone was pleased to see that the place card next to his read MIRABELLE CHANCE, although there was no sign of her. A parade of food and wine ensued.

They were halfway through their first course, a slab of fresh foie gras, when Mirabelle Chance finally took her seat. The gentlemen all rose to receive her, and Marcel introduced her to those at the table she had not yet met.

"I do beg your pardon," she said, with the slightest French accent layered over upper-class British English. "There was a line in the loo."

"There always is," Viv said, and everybody laughed.

"Now, Mr. Barrington," Mirabelle said, "since I know your name, it is time for me to learn who you are, where you come from, and everything else about you of any possible interest."

Stone laughed. "Well, I am an attorney," he said. "I come

from New York, and everything else about me you will have to root out, one piece of information at a time."

"Then I must work for my supper?"

"Only as hard as you wish to," Stone replied, "but before you start, I think I'm entitled to an exchange of information."

"All right," she said. "I am a Parisienne from my birth, though, having a British mother and an indifferent French father, I went to school and university in England, then I at first modeled, and now I design dresses, including the one I am wearing."

Stone looked her up and down. "You are very good at what you do," he said.

"Now, my turn to dig," she said. "Where were you schooled?"

"Within a few blocks of my home in Greenwich Village, at P.S. Six, at New York University, then at their law school."

"No further graduate work?"

"Yes, I got my Ph.D. as a patrolman and detective with the New York Police Department. I attended for fourteen years, but the degree is purely honorary." He nodded toward Dino. "That gentleman over there, whose name you will remember is Dino, was my partner as a detective, and he now rules the NYPD as police commissioner. His wife, Vivian, or Viv, as we call her, was a decorated detective before she retired to enter the private sector."

"My goodness, so many policemen. I feel quite at home, because my father, Michel Chance, is the prefect of police and the Cabinet, the most important of several prefects and roughly analogous to the position of Commissioner Bacchetti."

Marcel spoke up. "May I say I feel extremely safe at this table?"

"And well you should," Mirabelle said.

"And how did you avoid becoming a police officer?" Stone asked.

"That was left to my brother, who has risen through the ranks to the position of commandant, and is in charge of investigations in Paris."

"Until Dino's recent promotion," Stone said, "he held that position in New York—chief of detectives."

"Well," Mirabelle said, "now we have everyone's credentials."

"Not quite," Stone said. "Which university did you attend in Britain?"

"Cambridge," she replied, forking a considerable chunk of foie gras between her lush lips.

"I congratulate you," Stone said.

"Thank you, but your congratulations are late, since I earned my degree some fifteen years ago."

"My apologies for my tardiness. For whom do you design dresses?"

"I am strictly couture," she said. "I make dresses for clients, I do not manufacture them for the masses, or even for the elite classes."

"If you were a Frenchwoman, Stone," Marcel said, "you would know all this. Mirabelle is quite famous in her world."

"I never doubted it," Stone said. "Mirabelle, perhaps you

could tell me why there are two men in black suits across the room there"—he nodded—"staring at you."

"My father and my brother feel that, since I am of their family, I require police protection at all . . . well, at *nearly* all times."

"I'm glad there are exceptions," Stone said.

"And perhaps you could tell me, Stone, why the man and woman in gray over there"—she nodded—"are staring at *you*?"

"They are employed to see that I may do business in Paris without coming to harm."

"Since you are dealing with Marcel, I assume this is l'Arrington business of which you speak?"

"It is."

"Stone," said Marcel, "is the originator of the Arrington brand, having opened the first one in Bel-Air, Los Angeles. He also sits on the board."

"Along with Marcel," Stone pointed out.

"Well," said Mirabelle, "if I should ever need a place to sleep, I shall know whom to call."

"I am at your beck and call," Stone said, handing her a card, "and I hope I may be of service soon."

Mirabelle tucked the card into her bosom. "We shall see," she said.

TWO HOURS LATER, sated and suffering from jet lag, Stone and his party went downstairs to his waiting Mercedes van. It wasn't there.

Stone was about to call Rick LaRose when his cell phone vibrated. He glanced at the calling number. "Yes, Rick?"

"Your van has become unavailable," Rick said. "Get everybody back inside and wait for my call."

Stone herded his group back inside. "Rick LaRose's orders," he said.

"Oh," Mirabelle said, "there is my car outside now." She said good night to all, went outside and departed.

A moment later, a long black car appeared outside, and Rick LaRose got out and came inside. "We have another car for you," he said.

They trooped outside and got into the car. As they drove away Stone asked, "Whose car is this?"

"The ambassador's," Rick replied.

"And what happened to the van?"

"Don't ask."

S tone was awakened by the room service waiter early the next morning. For a moment he forgot he had left the order on the doorknob.

He let the man in, then got back into bed while the waiter set a tray on his lap, along with a copy of the *International New York Times* and one of *Paris Match*. Stone tried that, but his French wasn't good enough to read it, so he reverted to the *Times*. He switched on the TV and found CNN.

His phone rang. "Yes?"

"It's Rick."

"Good morning, Rick."

"Do you have the TV on?"

"Yes, on CNN."

"Turn it to the local news, channel two."

Stone switched and found a Frenchwoman gazing into the camera, producing a torrent of her language. "Okay, got it. What am I watching?"

"Just hang on for a minute."

"Have you planted something on TV, Rick?"

"No, but I got a tip to watch this."

The woman's image disappeared, replaced by that of a burning vehicle.

"What's this, a bomb in Paris?"

"No, that's your van," Rick said.

Stone looked more closely, but it was hard to tell. "And why is it on fire?"

"Someone is sending either you or me a message."

"If the message is for me, what is it?"

"If it's for you, I think it means, 'Pay attention this time.'"

"To what?"

"To the people who tried to kill you when you were last in Paris."

"The Russians?"

"Looks that way."

"Let's assume for a moment that the message is for you, instead of me. What is the message?"

"'Stop trying to protect Stone Barrington.'"

"What happened to the driver?"

"He was standing, leaning on the van, having a cigarette—he's not allowed to smoke in the van—and someone laid a cosh upside his head."

"Is he all right?"

"He's in our little clinic at the embassy, and he has a very bad headache, but the doc says he'll be okay."

"So, how are you going to react to this message?"

"By replacing the van. We have more than one. A black one will be there at noon to pick you up for your lunch date with Marcel duBois."

"How did you know I was having lunch with duBois?"

"I'm in the CIA, remember?"

"Oh, yeah, I forgot: you know everything."

"Near enough to everything—enough to put two men in the van this time: one to protect you and the other to protect him."

"Well, I hope your plan works. From what I just saw on TV, I don't think the air-conditioning could keep up."

"It'll be okay this time, I promise. You know, this incident is probably going to help us more than it'll hurt."

"How will it do that?"

"By telling Lance that our little operation here is a good idea. Lance likes learning that he was right."

"Who doesn't?"

"You're going to be getting another call this morning."

"From whom?"

"Mirabelle Chance."

"The last woman I met in Paris was one of yours. Is Mirabelle one of yours, too?"

"I'm working on that. In fact, you could be a great help to me."

"You want me to recruit her for you? I wouldn't know how to begin."

"She clearly likes you. We know that from her behavior at the dinner last night."

"I hope you're right. I certainly like her."

"She may raise the subject with you. I, and particularly Lance, would be grateful if you could help her move in our direction."

"What do you want from her?"

"Anything we can get. She's very well connected in Paris, beginning with her father and brother, and continuing down her client list, which is heavy with the wives and mistresses of government officials."

"Okay, Rick, if she asks me if she should become a resource for the Agency, I'll say, sure, why not?"

"Come on, Stone, you can do better than that."

"I can't promise that I will."

"I'll rely on your good sense. Gotta run. The van will be there at noon." He hung up.

Stone stared at the breakfast in his lap, congealing before his eyes. Eggs Benedict did not benefit from getting cold. The phone rang. "Hello?"

"Good morning, Mr. Barrington," Mirabelle said.

"Good morning, Mademoiselle Chance," he said.

"Are you free for breakfast?"

"I am, if we can do it here."

"At l'Arrington?"

"In the penthouse suite."

"I'll be there in half an hour. *Au revoir.*" She hung up.

Stone called down to room service to collect the tray and to double the order, then he got out of bed and into a shower and a shave.

S tone's doorbell rang, and he opened it to find standing there Mirabelle Chance, dressed to the gills.
Cheeks were kissed.

"Do you always dress so beautifully for breakfast?" he
asked, admitting her to the suite.

"Of course," she replied. "I am my own best advertising. Do
you like it?"

"You make that dress look gorgeous," he said.

"I'm not sure that I understand your language well enough
to know if that is a criticism of the dress."

"Not at all," Stone replied. "The dress would make any
other woman look beautiful."

"Again, I'm not sure . . ."

"I compliment the beauty of both you and the dress," he said. "Without reservation."

She blinked, then smiled. "Have you coffee?" she asked.

The doorbell rang. "I do now." He admitted the waiter, who set up the table on Stone's terrace. Shortly, they were seated, and Mirabelle had her coffee.

"Beautiful view, isn't it?" Stone said.

"That is the Luxembourg Palace," she said, pointing, "and surrounding it are the Luxembourg Gardens. And they are both very beautiful. How well do you know Paris?"

"Not as well as I expect to in a couple of weeks. What I need is a personal guide."

She leaned forward on her elbows. "Is that *all* you require?"

"The river of my needs is broad and deep," he said.

"So, then, it takes more than one woman to meet them?"

"Not necessarily. It just takes more than a personal guide."

"A multitasker, then?"

"If you want to be technical."

"Do you?"

"I would prefer not." The waiter, who had been rearranging the silverware, brought two plates of eggs Benedict from the hotbox below, set them in place, and whisked away the covers.

"*Bon appétit,*" he said, then vanished.

"Now we are alone," she said.

"No, we have eggs Benedict."

"Ah, yes." She dug in. "Tell me," she said after a moment's chewing, "what is your connection to the CIA?"

"I am a consultant to the Agency," Stone said.

"What does that mean?"

"It means that sometimes they ask for my advice, and I give it. At other times they don't, and I don't."

"Are you paid for this advice?"

"Only on a piecework basis."

"How much per piece?"

"I bill them by the hour. I am an attorney, after all, and that is our wont."

"You won't what?"

"It means our usual practice or desire."

"You bill the CIA for your desires?"

"No, I bill them for *their* desires. What is your connection to French intelligence?"

"None," she said. "They have so many—anagrams?"

"Acronyms."

"Ah, yes, acronyms. French intelligence has too many, and I would never know with whom I was dealing. I have been asked, sort of, to become associated with American intelligence."

"In what capacity?"

"As a conveyor of gossip, apparently."

"I suppose you would hear quite a lot of that from your clients."

"Constantly, but rarely anything that would amuse the CIA."

"You never know what might entertain them," Stone said. "Did you accept their offer?"

"Not yet. What is your advice?"

"Would it amuse you to associate yourself with them?"

"Possibly."

"Then accept, but negotiate the terms."

"How do you mean?"

"You are a businesswoman: whatever they offer you, demand more."

"Will I get it?"

"You will get some of it, that's what a negotiation is about: you rarely get everything you want."

"I nearly always get everything I want," she said emphatically.

"I'm not surprised. Perhaps I should hope that you don't want me."

"If I should want you, then God help you."

"In that circumstance I would prefer to handle the transaction myself."

She laughed.

"That's the first time this morning you've laughed."

"I don't laugh, unless I am *really* amused."

"Then I will take your laugh as a compliment—assuming that you are laughing with me, rather than at me."

"An interesting distinction," she said. "When I was at school in England I learned, with some difficulty, when Englishmen were being funny. I have had much less experience with Americans."

"Anything I can do to help," Stone said.

"Was that an offer of or a request for sex?"

"Not necessarily."

"You see! I think maybe that was meant to be funny, but I'm not sure. What does 'not necessarily' mean?"

"Not in every instance. It's best to go back a couple of sentences to my offer of help."

"What sort of help?"

"Almost anything you need."

"Almost?"

"It's best to reserve a little wiggle room."

"Wiggle? Is that like wriggle?"

"The same, only more colloquial."

She laughed again. "You are fun to talk with."

"I'm so glad, I would not like to bore you."

"I will let you know when you are boring me." She looked at her wristwatch.

"Ah, already," Stone said.

"No, no, I just have an appointment in twenty minutes, and there is the rush-hour traffic."

"Then you had better finish your eggs."

She pushed back from the table. "No, only half my eggs are on my diet. I must continue to be able to wear my own designs."

"Would you like to have dinner this evening?"

"Just the two of us?"

"I prefer conducting business during the daylight hours, reserving the evening for more intimate occasions."

"When and where?"

"Eight o'clock? At your favorite restaurant."

"Eight is good. I don't have a favorite, there are too many in Paris."

"Your favorite today."

"All right. Do you know Brasserie Lipp? In Saint-Germain-des-Prés?"

"I do."

"Eight o'clock then."

They rose, bussed, and she departed.

Stone sat down and finished his eggs.

The new black Mercedes supervan was indeed waiting for him in l'Arrington's courtyard at the appointed hour, and it got through the midday Paris traffic with few delays. Stone noted the second man up front, and he could see the short barrel of an automatic weapon protruding from the man's cradled arms. He found that reassuring but unsatisfying, since it apparently indicated that Rick believed any opposition would be similarly armed. If bullets started flying, he would prefer single squirts to spraying, even if the vehicle was armored.

The van was stopped at an archway for a security check, then allowed to drive into a courtyard, much like that at l'Arrington, but smaller. There were three large trees in pots arrayed against the walls, and next to each stood a man in black body armor, booted and helmeted, with an automatic weapon slung from a shoulder. The concrete tree pots would provide cover, he assumed.

Inside the front door of the office building of, perhaps, fifteen floors, he was stopped at a desk and required to place his right thumb on a sensor while gazing into a lens with his right eye. The equipment indicated its assent by displaying two photographs of him on a screen: one taken the year before and one taken just now. "Good morning, Mr. Barrington," a female voice said from the speaker. "M'sieur duBois is expecting you. Please take the elevator at your left to the top floor."

"Thank you," Stone replied to the mass of electronic equipment. Stone knew the building housed Marcel's business operations and that he lived on the top two floors. As the car rose a piece of music, a particular favorite of his, began to play: the Dave McKenna Quartet with Zoot Sims, playing "Limehouse Blues." The car reached the top floor before McKenna's piano solo was over, but as he stepped off the elevator, the music continued from unseen speakers. By the time Zoot began his soprano saxophone solo, he was seated in a comfortable chair, a perfect Bloody Mary in his hand, being told by a minion that M'sieur duBois would be with him shortly. He sat back and luxuriated in the wonder of Zoot Sims. Superb. The vodka didn't hurt, either.

Marcel tapped him on a knee as "Limehouse Blues" died. "*Bonjour*, Stone. Do not rise."

The Frenchman sat down beside him. Their view through a floor-to-ceiling glass wall was of treetops and a view across the city.

"Good morning, Marcel," Stone finally managed. "I am very impressed by the new wrinkles in your security system. I assume the police-like costumes and weapons of the men downstairs were chosen for a reason?"

"Ah, yes. After our difficulties of last year, your good friend Michael Freeman suggested that the presence of security be overt, rather than the subtlety of men dressed in blue suits with bulges under their arms."

"An economical and, no doubt, effective change. What about my thumbprint, my cornea, and my taste in music? Where did they come from?"

"The prints were unobtrusively harvested from your person last year," Marcel replied. "And the music was read from the albums stored on the iPhone in your pocket. Imelda—the name given to her voice—deduced which was the most-played track among them and played it for you. I rather liked it. Are the artists popular in the States?"

"The artists, unfortunately, are all dead, as are most of my favorites—Count Basie, Artie Shaw, Erroll Garner, Duke Ellington, Ella Fitzgerald, et alia. Fortunately, their work survived them."

"Ah, yes, the same with me. Did you and Mirabelle enjoy your breakfast together?"

"Once again, Marcel, you are well ahead of me. Yes, we did."

"And have you been enjoying your Blaise?"

"I drive it to my house in Connecticut on a road ideal for it. I think it goes too fast for the police to see."

"Ah, good."

"I have also enjoyed the performance of Frederick Flicker, and he and I have come to a more permanent arrangement. I'm grateful for your realization that I needed him."

"Every gentleman of any substance needs a gentleman's gentleman to take care of him. I have so much substance myself that I need three, in shifts."

"I can manage very nicely with the one," Stone said.

There was the tinkle of silverware from behind them. "And now, shall we have some lunch?" Marcel asked.

They rose and went to the table that had been set for them. Instead of courses, a small smorgasbord was wheeled out on a cart, and they chose what they liked from a dozen dishes.

"So much food," Stone said. "I hope what we don't eat will not go to waste."

"Don't worry, the kitchen staff are anxiously awaiting the return of the cart. By the end of their lunch hour, it will be empty."

Champagne was poured for them. Marcel raised his glass. "A Krug '55," he said. "I hope you enjoy it."

Stone enjoyed it.

WHEN THE TABLE had been cleared they returned to their seats before the huge window.

"Now," Marcel said, "I must tell you that I have had an offer for my stock in the Arrington Group."

"Is it from a Russian source?"

"It is from a corporation, benignly named. No name was attached to it."

"Then I think we will have to assume that the source is Russian, and that the name is Yevgeny Majorov."

"It was a more reasonable offer than I would have thought that gentleman would come up with, but I have the same suspicions as you. Should I explore it further?"

"Marcel, should you ever wish to dispose of your Arrington stock, I or my other investors will buy it from you for a better price than the Russians would give you."

"Oh, no, Stone, I don't want out," Marcel said. "I just wondered if we should toy with them a bit."

"Marcel, these 'gentlemen' would regard anything beyond a simple no as an encouragement, and they would become even more of a nuisance than they already are. My advice would be to have your secretary, on your behalf, write a short, blunt refusal to the corporation. Don't even sign it yourself."

"All right, I'll do that."

"It has been my experience in dealing with criminal elements who seek to disguise themselves in legitimacy, that if you give them so much as a bite, they will want the steak, and the bone, too, on unacceptable terms. They have already accompanied your offer with a violent attack: the CIA van that I and my party rode in to your dinner last night was destroyed while we dined. This is what they like to think of as the carrot and the stick."

"And how will you answer the loss of the van?"

"The CIA will answer, since the van was theirs, and I expect they will do so emphatically."

"Will that not escalate the matter?"

"I think the Agency will do it in such a way as to discourage escalation."

"Do you know how they will do it?"

"No, and I don't want to know."

The two men changed the subject and discussed the opening of l'Arrington in detail.

"I'm very impressed with my suite and with what I can see of the lobby and the exterior."

"By our opening next week, all will be perfection," Marcel said. "I assure this by throwing the first party in the hotel for the staff and the construction crews. They will bring their wives and girlfriends to dine and drink, and for their party, they will see that everything is perfect. Our party will be a couple of nights later."

Stone rose to return to his van. "Anything I can do at the hotel?"

"You might send a note to the manager with any suggestions, complaints, or requests that would make your stay more enjoyable. Guest feedback is the one thing we don't have yet."

"I will do so."

They said their goodbyes, and Stone returned to the sanctity of his supervan.

S tone was still feeling the effects of jet lag, so he had a nap, and when he woke, the Bacchettis were in the living room.

"We've ordered tea," Viv said. Dino merely rolled his eyes. The waiter arrived and arranged things, then left.

"Have you made plans for dinner?" Viv asked.

"I have," Stone replied. "Will you excuse me?"

"Yes, we have the welcoming dinner tonight at the Élysée Palace," Dino said. "It's our first opportunity to meet everybody before the conference begins tomorrow."

"It's Mirabelle, isn't it?" Viv asked.

"It is."

"Good, I'm glad you'll have the company of someone other than Marcel and us."

"That's kind of you, Viv." He knew she was thinking of Ann.

"Have you spoken to Ann yet?"

"Not yet. It's still early there. I'll try before dinner."

"What's going to happen with her if Kate is elected?" she asked.

"Everything," Stone replied.

"That doesn't sound good for the two of you."

"It's not. I'm going to have to get used to life without her, until she burns out on the job."

"Poor Stone."

"Don't pity me. We had a good run, and we may have another opportunity later."

The phone rang, and Stone picked it up. "Yes?"

"It's Rick. How was your ride today?"

"Perfectly satisfactory, thank you."

"Don't go anywhere unless it's in that van, you hear me?"

"I'm touched by your concern, Rick."

"I have my pension to think of."

"You're a little young to be thinking of that, aren't you?"

"Call it federal employee–itis."

"Any repercussions from last night's bonfire?"

"A small car bomb went off in a sheltered Paris street this morning. No one was harmed, but it made a lot of noise and smoke. I believe some windows were broken—the appropriate ones—and the facade of a particular building is going to need some work."

"So the message was delivered, but do you think they'll heed it?"

"I think they'll think twice before pulling such a stunt again."

"DuBois tells me he's had an offer for his Arrington stock from some corporation he's never heard of."

"And how did he respond?"

"I suggested he send a brusque negative reply."

"Good. I want them walled off."

"So do I," Stone said. "Rick, I didn't bring any self-defense equipment with me. Do you think you can supply me with something concealable?"

"When are you going out again?"

"Around seven-thirty."

"I'll see that there's a package for you in the van. Where are you going?"

"Out to dinner at a restaurant."

"Where?"

"Brasserie Lipp, in Saint-Germain-des-Prés."

"I'll see that you're seated away from the windows, and there'll be someone there to keep an eye on you."

"Let's not overdo it."

"When we don't overdo it, things happen. Witness the events of last night."

"All right, I won't complain further, just make it as unobtrusive as possible."

"Sure. See you later."

Stone hoped not; he hung up and called Ann's cell number.

The call went straight to voice mail. "Hi," he said into the void. "I'm in Paris and fairly recovered from the flight. Give me a call when you have a chance."

THE BLACK VAN was waiting in the courtyard when Stone came down, and there was a lump wrapped in tissue paper on the seat.

"Brasserie Lipp?" the driver asked, and started to move without waiting for the answer. The guard in the passenger seat handed Stone a small device.

"There's only one button," the man said. "Press it once two minutes before you need us to pick you up. Press and hold as a panic button for a rapid response."

"Thank you," Stone said. He unwrapped the package and found a small 9mm handgun in a holster that clipped onto his belt. His tweed jacket covered it nicely, and it didn't make a big bulge.

They pulled out of l'Arrington's courtyard and into the evening traffic.

"Hang on!" the driver shouted, and the van began to make quick turns down dark streets, then back onto the boulevards. Stone figured this was precautionary and not due to a threat. They arrived at Lipp at two minutes before eight, pulling up behind a black Mercedes S-Class with darkened windows. He got out of the van as Mirabelle got out of the Mercedes.

In a moment, they were inside, and the headwaiter immediately showed them to a cozy table well away from the windows.

"I don't know if this table is for me or for you," Mirabelle said.

"For the both of us, I think."

They ordered drinks and dinner.

T hey both ordered the house specialty, choucroute garni, which was a selection of sliced meats on a bed of sauerkraut, and beer, instead of wine.

While they waited for their food, Stone sipped his beer and had a good look around the place. He had taken the seat with his back to the wall, and he could survey the whole restaurant from there. His eyes stopped at a table across the room.

"Something wrong?" Mirabelle asked.

"I'm having a déjà vu experience," he said.

"Describe it to me."

"It's last year, I'm having dinner at this restaurant, and two Russian thugs are seated at a table across the way."

She looked into the mirror above his head. "Which ones?"

"The two in dark suits with shaved heads. An inordinate

number of the Russians I come into contact with have shaved heads."

"I see them," she said. "They look like their type, don't they?"

"They do."

"Well, they aren't going to start shooting in one of Paris's best-known restaurants. They'll wait until we're outside to kill us."

Stone laughed. "So we're two courses away from an ugly death?"

"But a famous one. We will be all over tomorrow's papers, and my father and brother will be on TV, separately, promising to destroy our killers."

"Why separately?"

"They don't like each other very much."

"How do they get along with you?"

"Better than they get along with each other."

"That must make for tense family dinners."

"There are no family dinners—at least, not with both of them in attendance. They take turns seeing my mother."

"And you're there for both turns?"

"Sometimes. I try not to always make it."

"Given the family business, you must have had an over-protected childhood."

"Once past puberty, yes. It didn't help that my brother, my only sibling, is ten years older than I. Boys with too much ambition for me were delivered beatings."

"Did that cut down on the number of your suitors?"

"No, it just made them stop coming to the house. I had to

meet them somewhere my father and my brother couldn't think of, or a girlfriend would pick me up and deliver me, on the way to her own evening out."

As their dinner arrived, Stone's cell phone began vibrating. He knew who it was, and he pressed the button that would send the call to voice mail.

"Do women often call you in the middle of a dinner with another woman?"

"It only seems that way," he said. "Anyway, it was my call being returned. I'll phone again tomorrow."

"She must miss you terribly."

"One hopes, but she is a very busy woman right now. She works for Katharine Lee's campaign."

"Ah, our papers have been full of the pregnant candidate!"

"What do the French think of it?"

"The women like it. The men think she should leave the race, but they are careful about telling their wives that. Do you know Kate Lee?"

"Quite well," Stone said.

"Is she carrying your baby?"

Stone held up a hand. "Don't say that, even in jest. You never know who's listening."

"You didn't answer my question."

"The answer is an emphatic *no*. I know her quite well, but not *that* well, and her husband is my friend, too."

"That would not stop a Frenchman."

"It wouldn't stop a lot of Americans, either, but I am not one of them."

"We have had some . . . *unusual* . . . first ladies," she said, "especially lately, but we've never had a pregnant one, at least not since Jacqueline Kennedy."

"Neither have we," Stone said. "I was at the press conference when Kate announced it, and the reaction of the media was pretty much nuclear in nature."

"Do you think it will help or hurt her chances of election?"

"The first poll taken after her announcement elicited mostly favorable responses from women and neutral ones from men. I think American men, like Frenchmen, don't want to argue the point with their wives. Their reactions in a bar with male friends might be very different, though."

"So, will it help or hurt?"

"I think it will help to the extent that it turns out the women's vote. If they respond, that could mean the election. The immediate effect is for the press to ignore her opponent and concentrate on Kate, which must drive the Carson campaign crazy."

"Well," Mirabelle said, "if it drives the other campaign crazy, it must be good for her."

They continued their dinner, but slowly, since they were talking so much. As Stone asked for the check, he saw the two men at the other table doing exactly the same.

"I'm going to pay in cash," Stone said, "and then I think we should run for it while the opposition is dealing with credit cards."

"I'm on my mark," she said.

S tone glanced at the check, threw some euros on the table, got up, grabbed Mirabelle's hand, and hurried toward the door. He glanced at the two bald men and saw one of them signing a credit card chit and the other rising and heading toward them. Stone hit the door running, passed the tables outside, and stopped on the sidewalk. No van. Then he remembered the panic button.

"Come on," he yelled, and started running through Saint-Germain-des-Prés. He groped in a pocket, then another but couldn't find it.

"Don't go down this street," Mirabelle shouted. "Too few people!"

Stone turned and ran back into the open plaza and into

traffic. A huge black shape appeared in the corner of his eye, and there was a screeching of brakes and a chorus of horns.

"Get in here!" a man shouted.

Stone turned and saw the van, the rear door open. He pushed Mirabelle inside and heard the door slam behind him. Through the window he could see the two bald Russians running toward them, looking annoyed.

"What happened?" the guard yelled.

"Two Russians," he panted.

"Why didn't you use the panic button? We had two men in the restaurant."

"Couldn't find it. Two Russians were there."

There was a banging on the front door of the van, and the guard's window slid down. He exchanged some words with someone outside, then closed the window. "Were the Russians two bald guys?"

"Yes,"

"Those were our people. You scared them to death."

"*Your* people?"

"Of course. What did you think?"

"I thought they were the Russians."

"You're getting paranoid, Mr. Barrington."

"I wonder why? I'm locked in an armored van with two armed men, two others are watching me in a restaurant. Why would I be paranoid?"

The man ignored the question. "Where to?" he asked.

"The Arrington?" Stone said to Mirabelle.

"I think we'll be safe there," she said sardonically. She

picked up her phone. "I have to call my car." She spoke in French for a moment, then put the phone away. "They'll follow," she said.

The ride home was much like the earlier ride—fast and down side streets. They were at the hotel sooner than Stone had anticipated.

STONE CLOSED the suite door behind him.

"That was quite funny," Mirabelle said.

"I'm glad you were amused."

"The sight of an American spy running from his own bodyguards must have amused any Russians present."

"Champagne?"

"Perfect."

Stone found a bottle of Marcel's favorite Krug in the bar fridge, opened it, and filled two flutes. He sat down next to Mirabelle on the sofa; she didn't move over.

"Listen carefully," he said.

"I'm listening."

"I am *not* a spy."

"So you say."

"I am an attorney. I am a partner in a New York law firm. As such, I sometimes consult for the Agency."

"You said that before, but it doesn't make any sense. Why would the CIA consult with anybody?"

"Sometimes they need an opinion or information from outside the Langley bubble. At least, that's my view: I've never asked them why they wanted me under contract."

"So you're a contractor?"

"Not in the sense of someone who does black bag jobs and shoots people in the head. I'm an attorney under contract."

"That's your cover story, isn't it?"

"There's the phone," he said, pointing. He gave her the Woodman & Weld phone number. "Call it and ask for me."

"Well, of course they would back up your story. It wouldn't be much of a cover if they didn't."

"What else can I do to convince you?" he asked.

She thought about that for a moment. "I don't think you can," she said at length.

Stone refilled their glasses. "Google me," he said. "You won't find a word about the CIA in the results."

"Oh, please."

Stone made a strangled noise.

"Tell me," she said, "what does it take to get an American spy into bed?"

Stone took her face in his hands and kissed her. "A kind word," he said, "that doesn't refer to the CIA."

"Please?"

"That will do nicely." He took their glasses in one hand and her in the other and headed for the bedroom.

A shaft of sunlight struck Stone's face as he slept. He threw up an arm, as if to protect himself from the paparazzi, but a check revealed the light to be coming across the neighboring rooftops. The bed next to him was empty; Mirabelle had snuck out early.

Stone staggered toward the bathroom, blinking to recover his full vision. The sound of the shower struck his ears. He walked into the bathroom and saw the lovely form of Mirabelle through the mist on the shower glass.

"Good morning!" she shouted over the roar of the water. "Please join me!"

Stone did so, and the rush swept away his sleepiness. Mirabelle had him in her hand, squeezing gently. "Is it awake?" she asked, biting him on a nipple.

He started. "It is now!"

"Ah, yes, I can feel it returning to consciousness." She bit him on the other nipple. "It's awake!" She put both arms around his neck and hoisted herself to him.

Stone cupped his hands under her cheeks to support her weight, freeing her hand to guide him inside her. "There," she said, nibbling on an earlobe. "There is where it belongs."

Stone pressed her against the tiles, then pressed home their union. He couldn't think of anything to say.

"Good, good," she was saying rhythmically. "All the way in. Yes!"

They came together noisily, and Stone's knees weakened. They sank to the shower floor, still entwined, and let the warm water run over them. A moment later they were toweling each other.

"I'm starving," she said. "When is breakfast?"

"I'll order." Stone picked up the bathroom phone and ordered, then hung up. "Twenty-five minutes," he said.

"Good," she said, taking him by the penis and leading him into the bed. "Time for one more."

They used the time well.

WHEN THEY had breakfasted and Mirabelle had dressed, he walked her to the door. "Goodbye, my spy," she said, kissing him. "You did not disappoint."

"I'm so glad," Stone said wryly.

"How about dinner in the country tonight? There are fewer bald Russians to frighten us there."

"I'm game."

"That you are. I'll meet you here at seven, and we'll take your tank to protect us from the automatic weapons fire."

"You make it sound so cozy," Stone said.

She kissed him and slipped out the door.

Stone was lying in bed with a second cup of coffee and the *Times* when the phone rang. "Hello?"

"It's Ann."

"Hello, there!"

"I returned your call last night but got only voice mail."

"I got your message, and I was waiting for it to be late enough to call you. There's a seven-hour time difference. Why are you up so early?"

"A dream woke me," she said. "I dreamed you were making love to another woman."

"My goodness." He couldn't think of anything else to say.

"It's all right if you make love to other women, Stone, just don't tell me about it."

"That's very generous of you. How is the campaign going?"

"Splendidly. Kate has crafted a stump speech for herself, including some funny stuff, and always a sly reference to the pregnancy."

"How's that going down with the crowds?"

"Like champagne. Carson's appearances, by comparison, are like a dose of castor oil."

"Fortunately, I've never tasted castor oil, but I understand the comparison."

"Fortunately, neither have I."

"Was announcing the pregnancy the right thing to do?"

"Absolutely. The very fact of it has kept the Republicans off balance since day one. And they can't say nasty things about a pregnant woman—their wives would kill them."

"How is Kate doing in the polls?"

"An average of a seven-point lead. Of course, that can evaporate in a flash, if she should stumble."

"Kate's not the stumbling type," Stone said. "How are you bearing up under the pressure?"

"I'm not sleeping much," she replied.

"More bad dreams?"

"No, I'm just always thinking—new ideas are flashing through my mind, and I can't seem to make them go away."

"Count sheep."

"Why didn't I think of that?"

"I'm always happy to give advice."

"I'm getting a lot of attention from the press," she said. "They usually mention you."

"In what capacity?"

"As my boyfriend, paramour, companion, or some other sly reference."

"I certainly don't mind the connection."

"Neither do I. Oh, my God!"

"What's wrong?"

"I have to get up and go to work."

"Give my best to Kate."

"I'll do that. Have a good day."

"I'll try. Call you later?"

"Perhaps it's best if I call you. I'm a lot busier than you are."

"As you wish."

She made a kissing noise and hung up.

Stone went back to his paper but didn't concentrate very well. He found the crossword impossible.

There was a hammering on the door. *"Entrez!"* Stone shouted.

Dino opened the door from the adjoining room. "Am I interrupting something?"

"Nothing left to interrupt," Stone replied. "She's gone. What are you up to today?"

"The head of the German intelligence service speaks at ten. Should be interesting. By the way, guess who's in from London?"

"I haven't the foggiest."

"You forget easily."

"Oh, God, is it Felicity?" Felicity Devonshire, with whom

Stone had had a long-running affair, was the head of MI-6, the British foreign intelligence service.

"Bright as a new penny, as the Brits would say. She sends her regards."

"Send mine back, and my apologies for not being in touch."

"What shall I tell her?"

"Anything but the truth—I'm not up to two women. Tell her I'm overwhelmed with the opening of the hotel."

"Gee, I hadn't noticed that."

"We have a board meeting this afternoon to hear about progress toward the opening."

"They're doing major stuff to the lobby and sandblasting the exterior."

"Good, those are the last things on the list. The rooms are ready for opening."

"You don't really need to be here, do you?"

"That's not what I told Bill Eggers. Actually, the board seems to value my advice. Perhaps it's because I don't give them much. Are you learning anything from your European colleagues?"

"Tidbits. We seem to be ahead of them in a lot of areas. I wish the Israelis were here, but they're not Europeans to the EEC. The Brits have a camera system all around their country that would be the envy of Big Brother."

"I'm sure you're working on that."

"We'll get what we need when Tom Donnelly is mayor." Donnelly was Dino's old boss, who was running for office.

"Then you'll have a free rein."

"We'll see. How's your evening looking?"

"Mirabelle is taking me to some restaurant in the country."

Dino looked at his watch. "Gotta run, there's a car waiting for me."

"What's Viv doing with her time?"

"Sitting at Mike Freeman's elbow at all the meetings, absorbing knowledge." Dino grabbed his briefcase, gave a little wave, and departed.

Stone got up and dressed—he wasn't sure what he was dressing for. The phone rang.

"Hello?"

"It's Rick. The ambassador would like to meet you."

"What on earth for?"

"I think she's curious about you. She doesn't really understand your relationship to the Agency."

"Neither do I," Stone said. "When?"

"How about right now? Your tank awaits."

"I'll go right down." He hung up, got into his suit jacket, went downstairs, and got into the waiting van. Twenty minutes later he was being escorted into the ambassador's office.

Her name was Linda Flournoy, he knew, and she was a billionaire's widow who had given a lot of money to the Democratic Party. About all else he knew about her was that she was said to throw great dinners and was fluent in French. She was already on her feet when he walked in.

"Good morning," she said, extending a hand. She was tall,

elegantly dressed and coifed, and looked ten years younger than her fifty-five years.

Stone shook the hand. "Madame Ambassador, how do you do?"

"Call me Linda," she said, waving him to a sofa and taking a seat at the other end.

"Linda, it is." He sat. "And I'm Stone."

"I've heard good words about you from the president and the first lady."

"They have always been kind to me."

"I witnessed the effects of what I heard was your influence at the convention," she said. "To hear some tell it, you were instrumental in Kate's getting the nomination."

"Reports of my influence are exaggerated. I was happy to help where I could. I would very much like to see Kate win the presidency."

"So would I," she said. "I'm having a good time in Paris, and I wouldn't mind being reappointed."

"You've been here, what, a year?"

"Fourteen months. Not long enough. Tell me, Stone, why is everybody trying to kill you?"

"I hope not everybody, but I seem to have run afoul of a bunch of mad Russians."

"So I hear. What do they have to gain by your death?"

"They want the Arrington hotels, but they won't get them, no matter what they do to me. There's an element of revenge involved, too."

"Revenge for what?"

"They think I was somehow involved in the death of a man named Yuri Majorov, who, apparently, was their leader."

"Him I know about. I heard it was of natural causes, aboard his own airplane."

"I heard that, too, but apparently Yuri's brother, Yevgeny, is a suspicious man, and he needs someone to be suspicious of. I seem to fill the bill."

"All right, I won't dig any more deeply into this with you, but I'm not getting a lot of answers out of the Agency's Rick LaRose, either."

"Rick may be as confused as I am, but he is doing his best to keep my hair from being mussed."

"I throw a lot of dinner parties around here," she said. "They're good business, and I can always use a spare man. May I invite you to something?"

"That would be an honor."

"You may have to put up with some boring women."

"Women are rarely boring," Stone said. "On the whole, I prefer their company to that of men, who are often boring."

"Tomorrow evening at eight, at my residence?"

"I'd be delighted."

"I hear it won't be necessary to send a car for you."

"Rick has seen to that."

"Lance Cabot spends money on the oddest things and seems to get away with it."

"I'm not surprised."

She stood. "Until tomorrow evening, then?"

"Until then. May I ask, what is the occasion?"

"I forget," she said. "The dinners all run together. Someone will hand me a one-page memo and a guest list a quarter of an hour before my entrance, so I'll know whom I'm talking to and why."

"Whatever it is, I'll look forward to it," Stone said. He shook her hand again and made his exit.

Mirabelle arrived at l'Arrington on time. "May I have a martini before we go?" she asked. "It will make the ride go faster."

"Of course." Stone went to the ice maker where he had stored the bottle of pre-mixed martinis and poured one into a crystal glass. He handed it to her and poured himself a Knob Creek.

"You should pack a toothbrush," she said, sipping her drink. "We won't be back tonight."

"What sort of restaurant is this?" he asked.

"You'll see."

He went and threw some things into a small duffel—a

favor of the hotel—and returned. She knocked off the last sip of her martini. "We're off," she said.

THEY GOT into the waiting van, Mirabelle spoke to the driver in rapid French, and he tapped an address into the GPS navigator. "Saves me having to give him directions," she said, leaning back into the comfortable seat.

"Tell me where we're going," he said.

"No." She looked out the window. "I promise you a good dinner and, if you play your cards right, as you Americans say, perhaps me."

"What more could I ask?" he said. He watched the city change into forest. "We're in the Bois de Boulogne, aren't we?"

"Shut up."

They had been driving for only half an hour when the van turned into a narrow, winding lane with thickly planted trees on each side. They stopped in front of an old cottage with a thatched roof and window boxes filled with flowers.

Mirabelle spoke to the driver again and got an argument back. "We'll be at the other end of the lane," he said in English.

She swore under her breath and got out of the van.

Stone grabbed his duffel and followed her. The van drove back down the lane. "What was the argument about?"

"He didn't want to leave us alone. I told him we weren't going back tonight, but it didn't seem to matter to him."

She opened the unlocked front door, and they walked into a cozy living room, where a small fire blazed in the hearth. There didn't seem to be a right angle in the room, but somehow, it looked like home.

"Hallo!" a woman's voice called from another room, then a plump, motherly woman came into the room and conducted a brief conversation with Mirabelle in their native tongue, and she left again.

"Was that your mother?" Stone asked.

"No, but she thinks she is. That was Marie, who has been the family cook for centuries."

"So this is a family cottage?"

"It is *my* cottage, bought with *my* money. My family has never been here, just Marie, and she is sworn to secrecy. It is my hideaway."

"Why do you need a hideaway?"

"My life is frenetic. Here is peace." She went to a corner bar and came back with a martini and a glass of bourbon for Stone. They sipped.

"This is Knob Creek," he said. "How did you know, and where did you get it?"

"I've seen you drink it, and I know a spirits shop that stocks it."

"You are good to me," he said, and kissed her.

"Tomorrow night I will take you to a grand restaurant."

"Tomorrow night, I'm afraid, I have to have dinner at the residence of our ambassador, and I was asked to come alone."

"Ah," she said, "the odd man."

"Exactly."

"She wants you for herself."

"No, she just wants an odd man. We met only today, in her office at the embassy."

"You wait—you will find yourself seated next to her, and there will be hanky-panky."

Stone laughed.

"This is an American expression, is it not?"

"It is a universal expression, I think."

"You will see, the woman has a reputation. She consumes men."

"I am shocked, *shocked* that you would speak of our top diplomat in France in such a way."

"And you are easy," she said. "Madame Flournoy will have her way with you."

"You make me sound helpless."

"She will render you helpless. She knows what she is doing."

"Where do you hear these things?"

"I've told you—my clients tell me everything. The ambassador is my client. She has spent much money with me and had many fittings. Women need to talk when they are being fitted."

"And it is men who have the reputation of talking about their affairs. Women are much worse."

"I will give you that, because it has been my experience. She will have your virtue, you will see."

Stone laughed loudly. "My virtue! Am I so maidenly?"

Mirabelle reached over and squeezed his crotch. "Before dessert, she will have this in her hand."

"I tend to be a one-woman-at-a-time man," he said.

"Why? You should have as many women as you want, who want you."

"I tire easily."

"Hah! You tire me, and that is not easy."

Marie entered the room as Mirabelle withdrew her hand. "Dinner," she said.

They got up and went into a kitchen, where a big La Cornue range rested against a wall. A table was set before another fireplace, and candles burned on the table.

"*Bon soir,*" Marie said, and left the room.

"Where is she going?" Stone asked.

"Home. She will come back tomorrow. I will serve us." She pointed at a chair. "Sit."

Stone sat. There was an open bottle of Château Palmer 1978, a favorite of Stone's, on the table.

"Decant the wine, please."

The cork had already been withdrawn. Stone stood, took the bottle and held it near one of the candles; as he poured, the neck of the bottle was backlit, and he could see when the dregs began to creep up the side of the bottle, so he could stop in time.

"Done," he said.

She took their plates to the stove and served them from the pots, then sat down. "Did you taste the wine?"

Stone poured himself a little and tasted it.

"Yes? No?"

"We'll drink it," Stone said. He poured them both a glass and they tucked into a dinner of boeuf bourguignon.

AN HOUR LATER they were upstairs in a feather bed, sated and a little drunk.

"I will wear you out," she said, "so there will be nothing left for the ambassador."

And she did.

Stone was wakened by a puff of chilly air; he got up groggily and closed the bedroom window. He was halfway back to the bed before he realized that Mirabelle was not there. She was not in the bathroom, either. A weak light from below was showing on the stairs, so, curious, he walked to the top of the stairway and looked down. The light was coming from the kitchen, and he could hear Mirabelle's voice, though he could not understand her French.

Still groggy from the dinner, the wine, and sleep, he tiptoed down the stairs and peeked into the kitchen. Mirabelle was standing there, naked, holding what appeared to be an antique shotgun, engraved, with exposed hammers. Both were cocked, and the shotgun was pointed at someone out of his view. He approached the door and peeked around the jamb. A man wearing black clothes and a black mask pulled over his head stood, his arms raised from his sides. Mirabelle was speaking to him in French that sounded hostile.

"What is going on?" Stone asked, stepping into the kitchen, and as he spoke he remembered that he, too, was naked. A low chuckle came from behind the man's mask.

Mirabelle took her eyes off her captured prey and looked at Stone. "I have him," she said.

Stone's eyes flicked toward the man, and he saw him reach behind his back for something. "No!" Stone said to him, holding up a hand. Everything then switched to slow motion. The man's hand emerged from behind him holding a semiautomatic pistol; Mirabelle turned toward him and pulled the shotgun trigger. The man's hand and his gun parted company; the gun was thrown toward the fireplace by the centrifugal force of his swinging arm; his chest exploded and his body flew backward and landed, flat, on the wooden kitchen floor with a loud thump. Only then did Stone hear the blast of the shotgun.

"*Merde!*" Mirabelle spat, at no one in particular.

"Well, yes," Stone said, recovering himself. He knew that much French. He was aware of the ridiculous appearance of two naked people, a shotgun, and what was rapidly becoming a corpse on the kitchen floor. Stone walked to her, took the shotgun from her hands, lowered the remaining cocked hammer, and set it on the kitchen table. He walked over to the man on the floor, pulled the mask from his head, and checked his pupils. Blown. He felt for a pulse at the carotid artery in the neck. None. "I think you'd better call the police," he said. "Tell them to bring an ambulance and a medical examiner, as well as a crime-scene team."

Mirabelle had begun to shake violently. Stone went to her and held her against him, and gradually she stopped trembling. She pulled away, then went and stood in front of the dying embers of the fire. "I can't call the police," she said.

Stone went and sat at the kitchen table. "You don't really have a choice."

"You don't understand," Mirabelle said. "If I call the police, my brother will be summoned as soon as they hear my name. He does not know about this cottage, and I don't want him to."

"The consequences of your brother's knowing about this cottage are small compared to those of not summoning the police immediately," Stone said. "Inevitably, your father will become involved, then someone at the police station or in his office will leak the story to someone in the press, and big headlines will be made. Very likely a criminal trial will result. Did you think we would just bury him in the Bois?"

She thought about it. "You are right," she said finally.

"Go and look at him," Stone said. "We have to know if you know him."

She went and stood over the man, staring into his inert face. "No, I don't know him."

"Is there any reason why anyone might send an armed man to your house?"

She nodded. "For you."

He nodded. "You have a point." He walked out of the kitchen into the living room, checking everything. No ransacking. He found the front door open and scratches on the lock. Outside, on the doormat, was a canvas satchel. He returned to the kitchen. "Very likely he was a burglar—his tools are outside. But nothing has been disturbed. I had better make a phone call before you call the police." He took her by the hand and led her upstairs. "Get dressed," he said, then found his cell phone and called a number on his Favorites page.

One ring. "LaRose."

"Rick, it's Stone. I'm at the cottage of a woman named Mirabelle Chance."

"The daughter of the prefect of police?"

"And the sister of his son, who is in charge of criminal investigations in Paris."

"What's happened?"

"She's shot an apparent burglar, as he was preparing to shoot her. I'm a witness."

"Where are you?"

"What is the address here?" he asked Mirabelle. She told him, and he told LaRose.

"Don't call the police," Rick said. "I'll be there in half an hour."

"Rick, we don't want the corpse to get much colder, and it's not a good idea to cover this up. We'll call the police in fifteen minutes. You get here as fast as you can, and I'll see what I can learn in the meantime."

"I'm on my way." He hung up.

"You stay here," Stone said to Mirabelle, "while I go downstairs and do some things. In fifteen minutes call the police, not your brother. After the first call, then your brother. He'll want everything to have been done by the book."

She nodded, pulled a sweater over her head, then sat down on the bed.

"It might do you good to lie down until they get here, but don't fall asleep. When they arrive, answer their questions truthfully."

"All right." She glanced at the bedside clock, then stretched out on the bed.

Stone pulled on some clothes and went downstairs. He turned on all the lights he could find in the room, including the one over the stove, then he looked under the kitchen sink and found some rubber dishwashing gloves and put them on. He walked over to the corpse and stood astride it, staring at the face. He hadn't seen the man before. He appeared to be in his mid-to-late thirties. No scars. He pulled up the black sweatshirt and checked the abdomen. Flat, no scars or tattoos. He pushed back the lips and looked at the teeth. All of them were white, even, very handsome. He bent over and felt the pockets of his trousers: empty. He reached under the corpse and felt the hip pockets: still nothing. He found an empty holster on the belt in the small of the back. He looked at the man's hands: no rings or tattoos. A cheap wristwatch on the right wrist. Nothing hanging around the neck. No ID of any kind. The man was a pro; the question was: What kind of a pro? Burglar? Assassin?

Stone returned the gloves to the cabinet under the sink, then went back upstairs. Mirabelle seemed to be sleeping. He stroked her pale face, and she jerked awake. "Time to call the police," he said.

15

Rick LaRose, amazingly, got there first, wearing jeans and a sweater, looking interested, but unflustered. He took off his shoes and walked around the corpse in his stocking feet. "He's a beauty, isn't he? What have you learned?" he asked Stone.

"Caucasian male, mid-thirties, six feet, a hundred and eighty, very fit, either extensive and expensive dental work or the most perfect natural teeth you've ever seen. No identifying marks, tattoos, or scars. No ID, no indication of nationality, had a manicure recently, no possessions, except a pistol, a holster, an extra magazine, the tool bag on the doormat, and a cheap wristwatch. Wears the wristwatch on the right wrist but is right-handed."

"Why do you think he's right-handed?"

"Because that's the hand that went for the gun."

Rick took another good look at the corpse. "Well observed," he said. "Part of you is still a cop."

"Always will be."

A claxon could be heard approaching from a distance, getting louder. Then it got softer.

"He's missed the drive," Stone said.

The claxon got louder again, then found the driveway and a car and an ambulance pulled into the forecourt, lights flashing.

"What an entrance!" Rick said, laughing. "It might be Inspector Clouseau!"

The gendarmes were quiet, quick, and all business.

Before they could speak Rick showed them an ID and jerked a thumb toward Stone and said something in French.

"And where, may I ask, is Mademoiselle Chance?" the officer asked in perfect English.

"Upstairs," Stone replied. "I'll get her."

"If you please."

Stone went upstairs; Mirabelle was asleep again. He woke her gently. "The police are here." She sat up and rubbed her eyes. "*Merde*," she said. That seemed to be her opinion of the whole business.

"Remember, tell them the truth." He took her hand and led her down the stairs to the kitchen.

The officer switched to French, and Stone didn't understand anything for twenty minutes. He hoped she was telling the truth.

Then the room got very quiet, and everyone turned toward the door. Stone followed their gaze. A man stood in the kitchen doorway: he was tall, had a gray crew cut, and was wearing a black leather trench coat. He lacked only an eye patch and a dueling scar to be good casting for a B-movie Gestapo agent. "Allo, Rick," he said. "How does it go?" His voice was calm and uninflected.

Rick shrugged. "It goes."

He walked over and looked at the corpse. "And what guest do we have here?"

His officer responded with a stream of French. The man stuck to English, an apparent courtesy to Rick. "Do you believe this to be self-defense?" he asked his officer. "Or do we have murder?" The man shrugged, as if the decision were not his to make. The man walked over to the table and looked at the shotgun. "My grandfather's," he said. He walked over to Mirabelle, took her by the arms, and kissed her on the forehead. "Are you all right, *ma petite*?" She nodded. "Is what my officer said the true thing?" She nodded again.

He walked over to where Stone sat.

"Jacques," Rick said, "this is Stone Barrington, an American visiting Paris and a prominent New York attorney. Stone, this is Prefect Jacques Chance."

Chance did not offer his hand. "What are you doing in this house?" he asked.

"I was a guest for dinner . . . and I fell asleep."

Chance managed a tiny smile. "And do you concur in what my sister has told the police?"

"I do," Stone said.

"Then you understand French."

"I was watching. Language was unnecessary."

The little smile again. "Of course. Mr. Barrington, did you shoot this man?"

"No!" Mirabelle said quickly.

"I was not aware that there was a shotgun in the house," Stone said. "I saw the man produce a gun. After that he was shot."

"What were you doing, Mr. Barrington, when the man was shot?"

"I was standing in the doorway, there." Stone pointed.

Chance turned to LaRose. "And were you watching, too, Rick?"

"No, Jacques, I arrived after the fact."

"And what brought you here?"

"Stone is a friend."

"So he called his friend, before he called the police."

"I called the police," Mirabelle said.

Chance sighed deeply. "So . . . everyone has the story straight. How very convenient."

Stone spoke up. "It's easy when it's the truth."

The prefect's cell phone rang; he answered it and spoke for half a minute, then hung up. "A stolen Fiat 500 was found on a road behind the house. It was an Abarth, so he liked his cars sporty. He walked through the Bois to get here, apparently. Perhaps we will know more when his fingerprints and DNA are run. Anything else from anyone?" He looked around the room, but no one spoke. "Then I bid you all *bonne nuit.*" He turned and walked toward the door. "I want the shotgun back in this house after it has been properly examined," he said to his officer as he passed, then he was gone.

The police loaded the corpse on a gurney and took it away. The officer gave them a little salute then followed it.

Stone noticed that there was very little blood left at the scene.

"Stone," Rick said, "your van awaits in the forecourt. I found it at the end of the drive. My men were asleep."

"I had dismissed them," Stone said.

"Then I won't have them shot."

"That's magnanimous of you, Rick."

"It is, isn't it?" Rick looked pleased with himself. "All right, everybody, let's all get some sleep." He gave them a little salute and left the house.

Stone took Mirabelle in his arms. "I'm glad that's over," he said.

"It's not over," she replied.

irabelle would not go upstairs until she had scrubbed the few flecks of blood from the floor and kitchen cabinets. "We will not shock Marie," she explained.

She fell asleep immediately, but Stone did not. Over and over he tried to explain the night's events to himself but could not. There were too many possibilities. As they were having a breakfast of eggs scrambled by Mirabelle, Rick LaRose called.

"Something Jacques and his boys didn't bother to tell us last night: the bag on the doorstep contained a few tools, but it also contained a length of rope, a black hood with no eyeholes, and a roll of duct tape. I don't think I've ever encountered duct tape in Paris. It's an American thing."

"So what are you thinking?" Stone asked. He didn't say it himself, because he didn't want Mirabelle to hear.

"He may have come to kidnap somebody," Rick replied. "I suppose he was strong enough to throw you over his shoulder."

"No," Stone said.

"Okay, he would have made you walk to his car, blind-folded."

"Perhaps."

"Easier to deal with her, huh?"

"Perhaps."

"I think I'd better do some looking into Mademoiselle Chance," Rick said.

"Why not?"

"I'll get back to you when I know more."

"Do that." He hung up.

"Was that your Rick?"

"Yes."

"What did he want?"

"He called to say he didn't know anything."

"Come now."

"Everybody's just guessing, even your brother. Who's next, your father?"

"I don't think Jacques will discuss it with my father."

"He seemed more concerned about the shotgun than any-thing else, except me."

"You answered him well. You told him we were none of his

business. Jacques would have appreciated your subtlety. I would have been blunt."

"We could still make the papers, but I think the policemen were too afraid of your brother to blab, so maybe not."

"Quiet intimidation is Jacques's, how do you say . . . ?"

"Stock-in-trade?"

"Yes, stock-in-trade."

"Mirabelle, do you have any enemies?"

"An old lover or two, perhaps," she said, "or one of their girlfriends. I don't think anyone is angry enough with me to send an assassin. What would be their complaint, an ill-fitting dress? I think it is more likely your Russians."

"You could be right."

"I am worried about you, not me."

"Thank you," Stone said. "Try not to worry at all. What did you mean last night when you said this wasn't over?"

"Nothing in particular. It is just a pattern in my life that when some event occurs, it always seems to be followed by other, related events. I've come to expect it."

"It's a pessimistic outlook."

"Then perhaps I am a pessimist." She looked at her watch. "I must go to work. Will you drop me there?"

"Of course. My chariot awaits."

STONE HAD NO TROUBLE falling asleep again in his own bed at l'Arrington. He awoke in time to make his board meeting, which included a tour of the hotel to inspect the premises. He thought Marcel's people had done a fine job of finishing their work on time. The hotel was beginning to look like what it was supposed to be.

LATE IN THE AFTERNOON, Rick called. "Your alleged kidnapper's corpse did not yield much," he said. "The man has never been arrested in Europe, his prints didn't ring any country's bell, and his DNA showed him to be of Western European origins, which could apply to half the population of the United States, as well as Europe, but that may indicate that he's not Russian. Oh, and his beautiful teeth were his own. All in all, the man's a cipher."

"Swell."

"By the way, the ambassador says she forgot to tell you that dinner tonight is black tie."

"Thanks for telling me."

"See ya." Rick hung up.

Nobody tried to kill or kidnap him that day, for which Stone was grateful.

Stone's van driver knew where the American ambassador's residence was without being told, and Stone presented himself to a butler and a pair of armed guards in the entrance hall, while some Marines looked on. He was scanned and passed through the metal detector on his second attempt, after his pen and his money clip had been deposited in a tray.

Having proved himself harmless, he followed the butler into a larger hall and blushed a little when the man loudly announced, "Mr. Stone Barrington, of New York City." Only a few people of the two dozen present bothered to glance his way.

After a brief discussion with the bartender, Stone was

rewarded with a glass of Knob Creek, selected from a dozen patriotic whiskeys among the embassy's stock. This being U.S. territory, ice was not in short supply.

He did not know a soul present, except the ambassador, who held court at the far end of the hall, surrounded by half a dozen gentlemen. The room seemed short of women, until Stone felt a breeze at his back; he turned and a tall, fairly slim redhead in a knockout green dress came straight for him, as the butler hollered, "Miz Holly Barker, of New York City."

Holly threw her arms around his neck, and he gave her a little spin while she cuddled there. "I thought you would be dead before I had a chance to come to your rescue," she whispered in his ear.

"I stayed alive only for you," Stone said. She felt warm and familiar in his arms. She was slimmer than the last time he had seen her, and she had at least six inches more of the red hair. "How good to see you in Paris! How long can I keep you here?"

"Well, if you should die, my instructions are to accompany your body back to New York, but until then, I am all yours. I'm staying at the embassy."

"Not while I have a large hotel at my disposal."

"Oh, can you get me into l'Arrington?"

"All the rooms are booked for the opening, but there is room in my bed."

"I accept," she said. "The better to guard you."

"Well," said a voice from behind them, "I see that either you two have met, or you are getting along way too well."

Stone turned to find the ambassador standing there. "Madame Ambassador, how good to see you again. May I present Ms. Holly Barker?"

The two women shook hands. "Ah, yes," the ambassador said, "yet another gift from Lance Cabot's merry band."

"I've never heard it described quite that way," Holly said, "but I'm sure Lance would take it and be happy."

"My lords, ladies, and gentlemen," the butler wailed, "dinner is served."

A pair of mahogany doors opened at one side of the hall, and the group meandered among the half-dozen round tables, looking for their place cards. Stone found himself next to Holly; the ambassador, to his relief, after Mirabelle's comments, was at another table.

A large slab of foie gras had already been delivered to each plate, and a waiter was pouring Mondavi Reserve wines from California. "Given the new California laws," Holly said, "I'll bet the foie gras is from New York State."

Introductions were exchanged with their dinner partners, and everyone fell upon the food, hardly bothering to chat.

The second course arrived, and the waiter announced, "Ladies and gentlemen, the main course is Georgia fried chicken, and it is customary to eat it with your fingers, so silverware has not been provided for this dish."

The Europeans at the table made positive noises and dug in. Stone turned to Holly, who had a mouthful of chicken. "Why are you really in Paris?"

"Tell you later," she mumbled. "God, this is perfect fried chicken!"

After only bones remained of the chicken, the butler came into the room. "M'lords, ladies, and gentlemen, please turn over your place cards, rise, and find your new seats."

Everyone did so and learned that they now had new tables. Stone found his card two tables over, and the ambassador was waiting for him to his left.

"Ah, Mr. Barrington," she said, "I've missed you. How was the fried chicken?"

"Superlative," Stone cried, "and the pâté before it."

"A gift from Governor Jerry Brown, of California," she said. "Apparently, he has to get rid of a lot of it." A hand squeezed his knee.

Uh-oh, he thought; how am I going to handle this?

But the ambassador was doing all the handling, and she was making progress up his thigh. Dessert came, announced to be blueberry pie from Maine, and at the first bite Stone flew into a fit of coughing. The hand was already at his zipper as he excused himself from the table, still coughing, and made his way to a men's room.

He hoped to God she didn't follow.

By the time Stone had returned to his table, dessert was gone, a small musical combo was playing, and everyone was dancing.

The ambassador took his hand from behind. "Dance with me," she said, and it wasn't a question. Stone took her in his arms, and they swirled to the music.

"Are you quite all right?" she asked.

"I beg your pardon, Linda, I inhaled some blueberry pie."

The music changed to a slow ballad. She moved closer; being tall, her crotch met his. "Ah," she said, "a response."

"It would be caddish of me not to," Stone said. He preferred this position to a hand under the tablecloth.

"We seem to be just the right relative heights," she said, sounding a little drunk.

"I can't complain," he said, thrusting a little to please her.

"You are an attractive man," she said.

"And you are an attractive woman."

"Why don't you stick around after the others leave?" she asked. "We can discuss our mutual attraction."

"What a good idea," Stone said. "Unfortunately, Ms. Barker seems to have Agency business to discuss, and she has pre-empted the remainder of my evening."

"That *is* unfortunate," she said. "Perhaps I should ring up Lance Cabot and have her recalled."

Stone shook his head. "People would talk, and we can't have that."

She sighed. The music ended. "On another occasion, perhaps?"

"I would enjoy that."

"I'll see that you do," she said, and was whisked away by another partner.

"May I have this dance?" Holly stepped into his arms. "What was that conversation about?"

"You. She suggested she might call Lance and get you yanked."

"Jealous, is she? Then the stories I've heard about her must be true."

"Oh? What have you heard?"

"That she was not unreasonably unhappy when she found herself a widow."

"She struck me that way."

"Would you like to hear what she's said to be particularly good at?"

"Whatever it is, I'm sure you are her superior."

Holly laughed. "I'm sure of that, too. Is it too early for us to get out of here?"

"Nothing could please me more."

"We'll see about that," Holly said.

Half an hour later Holly's clothes were hung in his closet at l'Arrington, and she was demonstrating her superiority to the ambassador. Stone responded in kind, and so it went for the better part of an hour.

THEY AWOKE in each other's arms and reengaged for half an hour before breakfast arrived. Holly ran for a robe before Stone opened the door to admit the room service waiter.

Shortly, they were sitting up in bed with eggs Benedict in their laps.

"So," Stone said, "what got you to this side of the pond?"

"Well, Lance has been pestering me to take some time off."

"Tell me, how many days have you not worked since he made you New York station chief?"

"Let's see . . ."

"Not a one, correct?"

"I am ashamed to say you are correct. So finally, Lance ordered me to Paris to cover your ass."

"What a wonderful human being Lance is!"

"Isn't he? Well, maybe not. I think he just thought I'd work better if I got laid now and then."

"He's a smart human being, too."

"I know I must be interrupting a liaison of some sort," she said. "Is there someone under the bed?"

"No, there is not. However . . ."

"I thought so! Who is she?"

"Well, I had no idea you were going to turn up, or I would have been, in Tallulah Bankhead's memorable words, 'as pure as the driven slush.'"

"Perfectly put, in your case. Now, who is she?"

"She's the daughter of the prefect of police and the sister of another highly placed Paris police commander."

"So, you're under constant surveillance?"

"Perhaps so. I haven't found any bugs in the suite, though."

"Shall we look for them?"

"No, let's entertain the listeners."

"I don't really mind your philandering, Stone—even when it's not with me. We are of similar natures."

"I know that, and somehow, it always makes our reunions important to me."

"And to me, too. It reminds me of how crazy I am to work so much, but I was so happy to get the job that I thought I should do it well. Unfortunately, doing it well is, all too often, a 24/7 job. Now tell me about these attempts on your carcass."

Stone told her about the roasted van and the shotgun incident of the night before.

"I'm impressed that she had the fortitude to fire when the time came."

"The lady is not lacking in fortitude," Stone said, "but I was impressed, too. I would have liked an opportunity to speak with the other shooter, though."

"So they know absolutely nothing about him?"

"Nothing, except what I told you."

Holly got out of bed, went to her luggage, and came back with a laptop computer. "Let's try something," she said, logging on to the CIA mainframe and opening the facial recognition program. "Let's see. Age, thirties. Height, six feet. Weight, one-eighty. Is that right?"

"Right."

"Did he speak at all?"

"He never had the chance."

"Hair color?"

"Light brown, I suppose. He had a rather severe flattop haircut."

"What was he packing?"

"The Beretta 9mm that's the standard army sidearm."

"Lots of those around. You said that he went for the gun with his right hand, but his wristwatch was on his right wrist?"

"Right. I thought that was odd."

"Let's type in 'ambidextrous,'" Holly said, and did so. "Any apparent skills?"

"Burglary and car theft," Stone said.

"There was no fight?"

"Not that I saw. Apparently, she heard something down-stairs and went down there with her grandfather's shotgun. I got there just in time to see it used."

Holly clicked on "search" and waited. She did not have to wait long. "Is that the guy?" she asked, turning the screen toward him.

Stone stared into a familiar face. "Holy shit, it is! How'd you do that?"

"The ambidexterity did it," she said. "Only about three per-cent of the population has that gift." She tapped some more and came up with another photograph, this one in the uni-form of a United States Marine, with a file attached.

"Name, John Simpson, no middle initial. White-bread all the way through. English descent, born in Gatlinburg, Ten-nessee, thirty-nine years ago. Attended the local schools, got his high school diploma, joined the Marines on graduation at seventeen, with parental permission, rose to master sergeant, two tours each in Iraq and Afghanistan— Uh-oh. Detached for special service four years ago—that means Special Forces or Navy SEALs . . ."

"Or CIA," Stone pointed out.

"Oh, Jesus," Holly said.

T he two of them sat in bed and stared at the file of
John, no middle initial, Simpson. "Is that all there
is?" Stone asked.

"In this particular file, yes," Holly replied. "His service
record ended when he was transferred to Special Operations,
and a new record was started. That file is heavily encrypted,
and only the director of Central Intelligence—and others at
his level in the various services—can retrieve it. That explains
why his fingerprints and DNA didn't produce a match."

"Wouldn't his whole service record be sequestered, then?"

"Yes, but we didn't request his record—we made him with
the facial recognition program, and I guess that was a back

door to his original service record. Watch." She started over on the mainframe and requested the army service record of John, no middle initial, Simpson. Immediately, she got a response: NO RECORD EXISTS.

"So, call Lance and ask him to retrieve the file."

"Can't you think of a reason why we shouldn't do that?" Holly asked.

Stone thought that over. "Because there's a chance that Simpson could be CIA?"

"Right, and if that's the case, Lance might know what Simpson was doing at your friend's house. And I don't think I want to ask Lance about that."

"I see. Suppose Simpson had retired from whatever special service he had been transferred to. Would that make his record more easily retrievable?"

"No, it would be permanently sequestered. I think you're thinking . . ."

"Suppose he left the service and became a freelancer?"

"Right."

"The question remains, a freelance what? I figured him for a pro when I looked him over, but I still don't know a pro what."

"Suppose he didn't leave his new service?" Holly said.

"Well, I don't think Army Special Forces or Navy SEALs would be conducting operations in Mirabelle Chance's kitchen," Stone said. "Or committing burglary and grand theft auto in Paris."

"Good point," Holly said. "So where do we go from here?"

"How about to Rick LaRose?" Stone suggested.

"Rick is a station chief, like me. He wouldn't have access to a sequestered service record any more than I do."

"Maybe not, but he was at the scene. That gives him a good excuse to ask Lance to retrieve the file."

"That raises another thorny point," Holly said.

"What's that?"

"If Simpson was working for the Agency in Paris, Rick, as the local station chief, would be aware of it, and he would know why. And if he doesn't know, it might be very embarrassing for him."

"And yet he seems as baffled as we are by the dead guy in Mirabelle Chance's kitchen."

"If I were in Rick's shoes, and I knew about an operation, it would be in my interests to seem to be baffled, too," Holly pointed out.

"God, I'm glad I'm only a simple, barefoot New York lawyer and not an intelligence agent. It's too complicated."

"Now you know why I work all the time," Holly said. "I have to figure out stuff like this."

"What the hell," Stone said. "I'm going to do what an amateur like me would do." He picked up his phone, dialed Rick's number, and put the phone on speaker.

One ring. "Rick LaRose."

"Rick, it's Stone."

"Morning. How was the dinner party?"

"Eventful," Stone said. "Rick, I think I've ID'd the corpse in Mirabelle Chance's kitchen."

"Oh, yeah? Have you come over all psychic, Stone?"

"Not yet. His name is John, no middle initial, Simpson, thirty-nine, U.S. Army master sergeant, maybe retired."

"Nah. If he had a service record, we'd have gotten a hit on his prints or DNA."

"Nevertheless."

"Nevertheless what?"

"Nevertheless, that's who the guy is."

"Where the fuck did you come up with that?" Rick demanded.

"I have friends in high places."

"Ahah! We're not talking about this on the phone. I'm coming over there." Before Stone could respond, Rick had hung up.

"Well," Holly said, "I guess I'd better put on my knickers."

HALF AN HOUR LATER there was a knock on the door, and Stone answered it. He and Holly had spent their time getting dressed and tidying the suite. Rick came in. "I knew you would be here," he said to Holly.

"Hi, Rick, how are you?" Holly asked. "How're things in Paris? How's the Paris station? How're the wife and kids?"

Rick went to the bar and found himself a bottle of fizzy water, then took a seat. "Things in Paris are just swell, the Paris station is a barrel of laughs, and you know I don't have a wife and kids."

"Mistress and kids? After all, it's Paris."

Rick ignored that. "What have you two been up to?"

"You'd better tell him, spy to spy," Stone said to Holly. "I might leave out something."

"All right," Holly said, and she told him.

Rick stared at them in wonder. "How long did all this take?"

"I don't know, eight or ten minutes," Holly replied.

"You just went online and conjured up a sequestered subject?"

"Looks like the facial recognition software is some kind of back door to some sequestered records," Holly said. "Anyway, we didn't get his sequestered record, just his old service record."

"That should have been sequestered, too," Rick said. "Somebody must have fucked up."

"Oh, that never happens at the Agency," Holly said, restraining herself to a slight sneer.

Rick sat, staring into his fizzy water.

"What's the matter, Rick? Are you seeing some sort of problem here?"

"Come on, Rick," Stone said, "cough it up."

"Cough *what* up?"

"You're the station chief, Rick. If this guy's Agency, you would know all about him, wouldn't you?"

"I don't know a fucking thing about him," Rick said, "and I very much doubt that he's Agency."

"So what was he doing in Mirabelle Chance's kitchen?" Stone asked.

Rick didn't have an answer for that.

"Why don't you call Lance and ask him to retrieve the guy's sequestered service record?" Stone asked innocently.

"I'll do that immediately after hell freezes over," Rick said. He looked at Holly. "Can you imagine what kind of can of worms that could open?"

"All hell could break loose," Holly replied.

"I imagine we're going to run out of metaphors in a minute," Stone said. "Not to mention clichés. What are we going to actually *do*?"

20

Rick pointed a finger at Holly. "You call Lance," he said.

"Don't point that thing at me," Holly replied, "I'm just a visitor here. I'm on vacation, sort of."

"You started this."

"Nope. We're on your turf, here, Rick. You're new at this, but you're going to have to learn what a station chief does."

Rick looked at his watch. "It's six A.M. at Langley," he said. "Lance won't be in the office yet."

"The Lance I know gets in at seven," Holly said.

"I'll e-mail him," Rick said, getting out his phone.

"Is that phone encrypted?"

"It is."

"All right, e-mail him. He'll get it when he arrives at his office, in an hour, or maybe he'll get it at breakfast. I expect he's used to getting e-mails at breakfast."

Rick typed a short message. "Done."

"That was brief. What did you say?"

"'Request sequestered service record of John, NMI, Simpson, thirty-nine, U.S. Army.' That's all he needs."

"Would you like some breakfast while we await a reply, Rick?" Stone asked.

"I've already had breakfast. I could use some lunch, though."

Stone looked at his watch. "By the time room service delivers, it will be lunchtime."

"I'll have a lobster club sandwich on rye toast, and a Heineken."

"Holly?"

"Corned beef on whole grain with mayo, and a diet Coke."

Stone ordered the food and a roast beef sandwich for himself, then hung up. "Half an hour or sooner."

"What'll we do until then?" Rick asked

"Anybody got a deck of cards?" Holly asked.

"What do you want to play?" Stone asked, rummaging through the wet bar snacks.

"I don't play cards, but I know a card trick."

Stone stopped looking.

"So," Rick said, "did the ambassador grab your crotch at dinner?"

Stone rolled his eyes.

"I rescued him," Holly said.

"Was he any safer with you?"

"Stop talking about me as if I'm not here," Stone said.

"Tell us something juicy from your station, Rick," Holly said. "We all have top secret clearances here."

"Juicy?"

"Juicy."

"Well, let's see: we caught a pickpocket who stole one of our officers' cell phones and was trying to sell it at the Paris Flea Market."

"That's what you call juicy?"

"All right, the ambassador grabbed Stone's crotch at dinner last night. That juicy enough?"

"We already know about that: surprise us."

Rick took a breath to say something, and his cell phone made a musical noise. "That's an e-mail," Rick said, digging the phone from its holster. He pressed a button. "It's from Lance," he said. "Message is as follows: 'NO FILE EXISTS.'" He stuffed the phone back in its holster.

"You're being stonewalled," Holly said.

"Maybe there's no such file," Stone said.

"We already know there's a file, we've read half of it."

"But not the good half."

"I'll give you that. What's your next move, Rick?"

"What's *my* next move? Why is it my move?"

"It's your station, so Simpson is your guy."

"He's not my guy—I never saw him before last night."

"Have you put any people on this?"

"Why should I put my valuable people on it? It's the Paris police's case, not mine."

"Don't you want to know what the guy was doing in Mirabelle Chance's kitchen?" Stone asked. "Before the Paris police find out?"

"My bailiwick doesn't extend to Mirabelle Chance's kitchen."

"Then what were you doing there last night?" Holly asked.

Rick pointed at Stone. "He called me."

"You're pointing again, Rick," Stone said. "When I called you, you came. Why?"

"I'm supposed to take reasonable steps to keep you alive," Rick said.

"*Reasonable steps?* That's all my life is worth to the Agency? What about extraordinary steps?"

"Getting me out of a warm bed in the middle of the night is an extraordinary step. I answered the call, and look where it got me. The Paris police think John, NMI, Simpson is my guy, and now they know *you're* my guy."

"They didn't know that before?"

"Not to my knowledge. Well, there was that incident last year when we thought somebody was trying to kill Lance, but they were really trying to kill you. They can remember that far back, I guess."

"So you lost nothing by coming to Mirabelle's kitchen?"

"I didn't gain anything, either." Rick's cell phone made the e-mail noise again, and he looked at it. "Oh, shit," he said.

"Now what?" Holly asked.

"Bad news: Lance wants me on a secure video conference at the station in an hour."

"Oh, goody!" Holly laughed.

"The good news is, he wants you there, too."

"Not me?" Stone asked. "I feel left out."

"Oh, all right, you can come, too. Where's my sandwich?"

An hour later, lunched, hunched over a conference table, and nicely groomed, they sat and
stared at a large blank screen in a double-
soundproofed, double-doored room.

"He's six minutes late," Stone said, consulting his watch.
"How does this go?"

"It goes when Lance gets around to it," Rick said.

The screen suddenly came to life, and Lance Cabot sat,
glowering at them. "I heard that, Rick," he said.

"Only joking, boss," Rick replied quickly.

"What the hell is going on over there?" Lance demanded.

"Where would you like me to start?" Rick asked.

"Start with the John, no middle initial, Simpson part."

"Well," Rick said, "late last night—or perhaps more accu-
rately, in the middle of the night—Mr. Simpson took a shotgun

round to the chest from a weapon held by Mirabelle Chance. It happened in her kitchen, and Stone was a proximate witness."

"And what was Stone doing in the kitchen of the daughter of the prefect of police in the middle of the night?"

"Stone?" Rick said. "You want to take that one?"

"Lance," Stone said, "you have a fevered imagination—use it." Stone, as a non-Agency employee, felt no need to kowtow to Lance Cabot.

"Jesus God," Lance said. "Is there no woman you won't take to bed?"

"I'll have to think about that," Stone said.

"There seem to be times, Stone, when you don't think at all."

Stone let that one go. "As long as we've got you on the . . . line, Lance, who the hell is John, no middle initial, Simpson?"

"I find," Lance replied, "somewhat to my consternation, that Mr. Simpson is an employee of this service, attached to the Berlin station as a handyman."

"Plumbing and electrical?" Stone asked. "Does he do windows?"

"All of the above," Lance replied. "The question is, what the hell was he doing in Mirabelle Chance's kitchen?"

"He was costumed as a B-movie burglar," Stone said, "in black, mask and all, and he left a stolen car parked outside. Oh, and he had a loaded Beretta in his hand and an extra magazine in a holster."

"Did he make any vocal noises?" Lance asked.

"He was unable to sing," Stone said. "Or breathe. He also could not work up a pulse."

"And where is Mr. Simpson now?"

"In a storage locker at the Paris morgue, I presume, or wherever the French deposit unwelcome corpses."

"Has a medical report been issued?" Lance asked.

"It has, Lance," Rick said. "Cause of death, shotgun wound to the chest. No scars, tattoos, or other identifying marks."

"They haven't ID'd him?"

"Not unless they have access to sequestered records," Rick said.

"Speaking of that," Lance said, "will one of you kindly tell me how you got to his record?"

Holly spoke up. "Lance, I ran our recognition software for Stone to have a look at, and Simpson popped up."

"Employing what criteria?"

"Stone's description of the man, plus indications of ambidexterity."

"What indications?"

"He was wearing his wristwatch on his right hand, yet he pulled his gun with the same hand. There's a contradiction there—the right-handed commonly wear their watches on their left wrists."

"How peculiar of you to think of that, Holly. I'll bet that little anomaly is what blew you through a back door of the software. Incidentally, the loud noise you just heard was the sound of that back door slamming. *That* won't happen again."

"Lance," Holly said, "I expect you've already spoken to the Berlin station chief. Was he enlightening?"

"Enlightening? The man was aware of Mr. Simpson only

in name on a list of employees. He's never spoken to the man, or even seen him. Incidentally, that gentleman is on the way home on a slow cargo aircraft, for consultations."

Stone spoke up again. "Underworked handymen sometimes seek additional employment," he pointed out. "Did the gentleman from Berlin, perhaps, shed any light on whom Mr. Simpson might be doing windows for?"

"He did not," Lance said, "being hardly aware of the existence of his minion. His deputy has now, however, been stirred to action, and I expect a report before the day is out."

"Shall we await further news from Berlin, then?" Rick asked.

"Certainly not. Consider yourself stirred to action, as well. I want to know how and why an Agency employee met his end on the kitchen floor of the daughter of the prefect of Paris police, and I expect the prefect does, too. I anticipate a hot call from him momentarily, demanding satisfaction."

"Lance," Rick said, "I don't think the prefect has any reason to believe that Simpson might be ours, or even Simpson."

"The absence of evidence will not affect his assumptions," Lance said. "Call me when you know more, and you had better know more soon." The screen went black.

"Well," Holly said, "that was as mad as I've ever seen Lance, and I've seen him mad more often than I like to remember."

"He'll get over it," Stone said.

This observation was met with derisive laughter from his companions.

Stone's cell phone was ringing as he let himself into his suite at l'Arrington. "Allo," he said in his best French accent.

"Allo, yourself," Mirabelle said.

"Good morning."

"*Bonjour.* Is Madame Flournoy still there?"

Stone summoned up some outrage. "I don't know what you mean."

"Didn't she follow you home last night? I've had reports."

"Your intelligence is unreliable. Madame Flournoy slept in her own bed last night, to the best of my knowledge."

"So you fucked her in the residence, then left? How caddish."

"You are—how do we say in *Anglais*? Leaping to delusions?

"I have leapt to all sorts of *conclusions*," Mirabelle said. "My reports also include mention of a lady from New York."

"She is a civil servant, in town on official business."

"So you are now 'official business'?"

"Sometimes," he said, because he couldn't think of anything else to say.

"A weak response. You are losing your touch, M'sieur Barrington."

"To what do I owe the honor of this call, apart from undue criticism of my motives and actions?"

"You and I cannot see each other anymore," she said.

A wave of relief swept over Stone. He had been unable to think of a way out, but she had saved him the trouble. "I am desolated," he said.

"Funny," she said, "you sound relieved."

"Far from it," he lied.

"I suppose you would like a reason? You Americans are always looking for reasons, even when there aren't reasons."

"That's because we know there are always reasons."

"I had an unpleasant conversation with my father this morning," she said.

"I hope I was not the cause of any unpleasantness between the two of you."

"My father has, as you neatly put it, leapt to conclusions, and he has concluded that your presence in my home, along with that of Rick LaRose and an unidentified corpse, are somehow related. He is probably on the phone to Washington as we speak."

"Ummm," Stone replied.

"I expect you will be hearing from whoever answers the phone."

"Does the corpse remain unidentified?" Stone asked, anxious to change the subject.

"Mystifyingly so, which adds to my father's suspicions about Americans. He tends to regard any mystifying circumstance as evidence of American meddling in French affairs."

"That is ungenerous of him."

"In any case, he has decided that my continuing to canoodle—this is the correct word, yes?"

"As far as it goes."

". . . with an American spy is not in the interests of France."

"I never knew that France was interested."

"By 'in the interests of France,' I mean in my father's opinion."

"Ah."

"Where his opinion is involved, he tends to broaden his scope to include the nation."

"That is magnanimous of him."

"I should say that I do not always strictly follow my father's wishes."

"Oh?"

"Sometimes my daughterly desires outweigh his fatherly advice. On those occasions you and I may happen to meet."

"How will I know when such an occasion arises?"

"I will communicate this to you."

"I will be all ears."

"I may not employ your ears in my communication."

"I will give deep thought to whatever that means."

"Until then, *au revoir.*" She hung up.

He had hardly hung up when Holly let herself into the suite. She pecked him on the lips and sank into a chair. "What a morning!" she exhaled.

"Have you and Rick found a way to meet Lance's, ah, request for further information on Mr. Simpson?"

"On reflection," she said, "Rick and I have decided that the matter of Mr. Simpson is between Lance and the Berlin station chief. Lance was just using us as whipping boys, until he could get his hands on the poor son of a bitch."

"Did you and Rick express these thoughts to Lance?"

"Certainly not. Do you think we're crazy?"

"Possibly."

"I simply lent Rick the wisdom of my long experience with Lance and his temper, and he seemed to appreciate my advice."

"I'm sure Rick is smart enough to appear that he is hanging on Lance's every word."

"We'll see," Holly said.

"I expect we shall."

"Tell me," she said, "I've been told that this city is a place where a girl can find a frock to wear to a party."

"I've heard that myself. I hope the party you're referring to is the grand opening of l'Arrington and that you are accompanying me."

"I was hoping you were hoping that. Where should I start the hunt?"

"Google 'party frock, Paris,' and a world will open up to you."

"No personal recommendations?"

"Chanel? Armani? Ralph Lauren? I believe they all do business here, along with several dozen other designers. Shall I arrange a hotel Bentley for you?"

"That would be gallant of you."

"How about a personal shopper?"

"What a good idea! Would you like to act in that capacity?"

"I fear that I am a poor judge, until I actually see the frock worn at a party. I can't stay awake in fancy shops." He picked up the phone and spoke to the concierge. "There," he said, hanging up. "Your car and your shopper will be ready in an hour. How may I entertain you until then?"

Holly stood up, unzipped her skirt, and let it fall to the floor, exhibiting a garter belt and stockings, but no knickers, then she sank into her chair and parted her legs, revealing a fresh Brazilian. "Improvise," she said.

And he did.

23

Holly sat back in the comfortable rear seat of the Bentley Mulsanne and sighed deeply. During the past months she had achieved a new high in unrequited randiness, something she had always relied on Stone to relieve, and he had never disappointed. She was alone in the rear seat; the driver and her personal shopper, Monique, occupied the front.

"Where would you like to go first?" Monique asked.

"You choose," Holly replied. "And please excuse me, but I must make a phone call." She found the switch that raised the glass panel between them and dialed a number on her cell.

"Research, this is Brian."

"Brian, this is Holly Barker. Why aren't you working?"

"Oh, I ah, I mean, I *am* working, Ms. Barker."

"Relax, I'm just messing with you."

"Oh, all right. How may I help you, Ms. Barker?"

"You can begin by calling me Holly, like everybody else but you."

"All right. Holly."

"Write down this name: John, no middle initial, Simpson."

"Got it."

"This man is an ex–Army NCO, currently assigned as a handyman in our Berlin station, at least, currently until last night, when he died. I managed to get a look at his army service record, which should have been and by now is sequestered, so you can't call it up. However sequestered it may be, it does not contain every fact of the man's life, and that is what I want to know."

"*Every* fact of the man's life?"

"That is only slightly hyperbolic. I want to know everything that can be found in a few hours. I want to know about his years in grade school, in high school, his church, if he had one, his hometown newspaper, and his school annual. I want to know about his academics and his athletics. I want to know who he lost his virginity with and if he knocked her up, and if so, what he did about it. I want to know everything his friends know about him, and his teachers and coaches, too."

"How long do I have?" Brian asked.

"What time is it there?"

"Nine twenty-one."

"You have until nine twenty-one tomorrow. I want it all e-mailed to me, and I may call you for more. Got it?"

"Got it."

"Have a good time." She hung up and lowered the glass partition. "Sorry about that, Monique. Where are we headed?"

"To Chanel, in the Avenue Montaigne. There are a number of other fine shops in the same street."

"Is Ralph Lauren there?"

"No, his store is in the Boulevard Saint-Germain."

"Let's be sure and go there after Chanel. His stuff is gorgeous, and it fits me."

"*D'accord.*"

CHANEL WAS A BUST; the fabrics seemed heavy, and things hung on her body like shrouds. She was shocked to find that a simple party top was €7000! Holly was not short of money, but she wasn't short of good sense. "On to Boulevard Saint-Germain," she said to the front seat of the Bentley.

AT RALPH LAUREN, everything fell into place. She found a green dress that went with her auburn hair and gave her very nice breasts a free rein, and she found a white double-breasted dress that you could see coming a block away and never forget. She didn't ask the prices, and she signed the credit card chit without looking at it. She also found some sensational fuck-me shoes, a knockout coat, and a new piece of luggage to hold all the things she was going to take back to New York. What would the folks at the New York station say if they could see her with all this stuff? They thought she was a grubby, workaholic nerd—which, of course, she was—but she harbored an inner babe that had to get out once in a while, and Paris was an awfully good place to cut her loose. She rode back to l'Arrington a happy girl.

STONE WASN'T THERE when she returned. She put away her purchases and checked her e-mail. Brian, bless his heart, had been on the job. He summarized:

"Johnny Simps, as he was called, was born and raised in a small Georgia town called Delano, and he was, from all accounts, a nasty little shit from the time he could toddle. He tortured small furry animals and any kid who was smaller than he was, which was most. In high school he was strikingly handsome—see the yearbook photo—but I talked to half a dozen of his schoolmates, and nobody had a good word to say about him. He was a pretty good high school quarterback—not good enough for college—who loved to play dirty and cheat, if he could. I don't know how you figured it out, but he did get a girl pregnant in high school: she said it was rape, he said, consensual, and he got two older girls to beat her up. A judge ordered him to join the military or go to prison.

"According to a friend of hers, the girl lost the baby but got herself together, got a scholarship to college, and was salutatorian of her class. She did a cosmetic start-up during her twenties, and sold the business for a hundred and twenty million dollars in her thirties, and she's now running her own business software company.

"Her friend swears she hired three guys to beat the shit out of Johnny Simps, and he arrived at basic training pre-wounded. Weirdly, he found a home in the army and straightened himself out. He had leadership skills and was promoted. He was also a crack shot with all sorts of weapons, and when he applied for Special Forces he got in and did well. An Agency officer spotted him in Afghanistan and encouraged him to apply, and he was accepted quickly. We don't have a record, of course, because that's sequestered, but the guy who recruited him said he did well at the Farm and afterward, even though he had a cruel streak, which his superiors overlooked. Says he was smart and street-smart and could run a team. His big fault was he was bad at languages, which, along with his lack of higher education, kept him at low-level tasks. He had no compunctions about wet work.

"I could spend more time on this, but I don't think it would be productive. Tell me what you want me to do."

Holly wrote back: "Brian, you done good, and it's enough. See you in a couple of weeks." She logged on to the Agency mainframe, called up Brian's record, and wrote a glowing addendum, resolving to promote him when she got back.

She called Rick LaRose. "You got anything new on John, no middle initial, Simpson?"

"Uh, something came up. I haven't even started."

"Never mind, I think I've got enough to tell you that he was a tough piece of work who didn't give a shit for anybody but himself. He did low-level wet work because it was all he was suited for, and he probably kept out of his station chief's way. I suppose he could have been freelancing for anybody who came along, but he knew how the system worked, and I don't think he would have left Berlin for Paris, except for somebody he knew and had probably worked with or for. You know anybody in Berlin?"

"Yeah, I know a guy in that station. He was fairly senior in Paris when I first got here."

"You trust him?"

"I know he's not a bad guy."

"Can he keep his mouth shut?"

"Yeah, I believe he can."

"Then get ahold of him, and the two of you find out who Simpson was working for and what he was sent here to do. I'm forwarding you an e-mail from one of my research people in New York that will give you some early background on the guy. It's not pretty. You and your buddy fill in the time since."

"I'm on it," Rick said.

24

Ron Spencer got off the C17 at Andrews Air Force Base and pulled the plugs from his ears, which were still ringing. He had reposed on web seating for the ten hours from Berlin, and his back ached almost as much as his ears. There was a car, or rather a ratty van, waiting for him. He threw his duffel into the rear seat and was driven directly to Langley.

"No time for a shave and a shower?" he asked his driver.

"My orders are straight to Langley, no stops. You'll be met." He made a cell call. "One hour," he said, then hung up.

Spencer was met in the big entrance hall to headquarters, walked past the wall of stars, representing CIA officers killed in the line of duty, and taken down to a sub-basement, to a small, bare room with a large mirror covering most of one wall. He had no doubt that this was going to be an interrogation, and that observers sat on the other side of the one-way mirror.

He was kept waiting there for a long time, no coffee, no chat, no toilet. He checked, and the door was locked. Forty minutes later a tall, gray-haired mustached man in an ill-fitting suit walked into the room, dropped a thick file—his, he assumed—on the steel table with a thump, and started talking before he was in the opposite chair.

"Who the fuck is John, no middle initial, Simpson, and why the fuck did you hire him?"

"Who are you?" Spencer demanded.

"None of your goddamned business. Answer the question."

"What question was that?"

"Don't annoy me, son, or you'll spend the next week in this room."

"I didn't hire Simpson. He turned up on the list of station employees I was given on my third day as chief."

"Who hired him?"

"I've no idea. He was assigned—I assumed from Langley."

"*Assumed?* Is that how you ran the station? *Assuming?*"

Spencer noticed that he had spoken in the past tense. "Did you ever run a station?"

"Three of them, and I'll ask the questions here."

"Did you interview every man and woman on the station staff?"

"I did, and I said I'll ask the questions. Why didn't you interview him?"

"Because he was a handyman, and I was a station chief. It was my deputy's job."

"What did your deputy tell you about Simpson?"

"That he was good at doing what he was told."

"Did you ever send Simpson to Paris for any reason?"

Spencer opened his mouth to say no, then reconsidered. "I sent a four-man team to Paris once—a handyman was among them, and it could have been Simpson."

"Who was the team leader?"

"A Frenchman named Jean-Noël Ragot."

"Why was a Frenchman working Berlin?"

"He was raised in the States since childhood: French father, German mother. He was trilingual and good at his work. I relied on him."

"And he took Simpson to Paris?"

"Maybe. I didn't ask. Why don't you ask him? He's still in Berlin."

ON THE OTHER SIDE of the mirror, Lance Cabot picked up a phone. "Get me the Berlin station," he said. "I don't care what time it is, I want to speak to an officer named Jean-Noël Ragot, wherever he is."

———

"WHAT WAS the purpose of sending a team to Paris?" the interrogator asked.

"I don't know that you're cleared to know," Spencer replied.

"I'm cleared to know whatever you know."

"I worked in the Paris station for fifteen months, ten years ago. While I was there I got friendly with a source in the Paris police."

"Friendly? Did you recruit him?"

"Sort of."

"What the fuck does that mean?"

"He was never on the books. I never wrote down his name, we exchanged information when it was good for both of us."

"Did you record or make notes on your meetings with him?"

"I made notes, but without mentioning his name. He was too smart to let himself be recorded."

"What was his rank and name?"

"He was a *capitaine*, and I promised him never to reveal his name to anyone."

"Don't hand me that horseshit! Don't you know where you are and how much trouble you're in?"

Spencer slammed a palm down on the table. "I know exactly where I am, who I am, and what I'm going to tell you, if I feel like it. What I don't know is who you are and on what authority you're asking me to blow a man I gave my word to."

The man opened his mouth to speak, but a buzzer went off, and he stopped. He got up, took the file on the table, and, without another word, walked out of the room, slamming the door behind him.

Spencer leaned back in his chair and yelled at the mirror: "I want to see the director now, and I want some coffee, black!"

Nothing happened for five minutes, then Lance Cabot walked into the room with a coffee mug in his hand, set it on the table, and arranged himself in the chair opposite. "Good morning, Ron," he said pleasantly. "Did you have a good flight?"

Spencer picked up the mug and sipped the coffee before he replied. "Good morning, Director. No, I did not have a good flight."

"Let's talk a little about your old job in Paris," Lance said.

HALF AN HOUR later Lance said, "There's a car waiting for you downstairs that will take you to the Four Seasons Hotel, in Georgetown. Get some sleep, have something to eat, get laid, if you can. You have a business-class seat to Berlin on the ten A.M. Lufthansa flight from Dulles tomorrow morning. Go back to work, and tell everyone in the station I said hello." Lance got up and left the room; a moment later, the escort took Ron Spencer downstairs and put him in the rear seat of a Lincoln Town Car.

Spencer was shaking as he got into the car. He did deep breathing exercises all the way to the hotel.

S tone awoke to the sound of the shower running, then he dozed off again. When he came to, Holly was bending over him, and she was, disappointingly, dressed. "You were just what a girl needed last night," she said.

"Always glad to be of service," he replied. "Why are you dressed so early? Are my services no longer desired?"

"They are, but Rick LaRose called, and I've got to run over to the embassy for a while," she said. "I'll be sure and be back for dinner. Book us somewhere special."

"Done," he said, then went back to sleep.

———

HOLLY TOOK a cab to the embassy and let herself in through the side door with her ID card. She identified herself to a guard in a glassed-in cage, then entered the Paris station of the Central Intelligence Agency and walked briskly to the station chief's office. "He's with someone," Rick's secretary said, then Rick opened his office door and waved her inside.

"Good morning." he said. "Thanks for coming over. Holly Barker, meet Jean-Noël Ragot of the Berlin station." A tall, heavily built man in his forties stood. "Hi, Holly," he said.

"Jean-Noël is the man I told you about," Rick said. "We served together in this station some years ago."

"Hello, Jean-Noël," Holly said. "What brings you to Paris?"

"I don't know," Ragot replied.

Rick spoke up. "Jean-Noël got a call from Lance Cabot yesterday, ordering him here."

"He didn't say why," Ragot added.

"Do I detect an accent?" Holly asked.

"Probably more than one," Ragot replied. "I have a French father and a German mother, but I was raised in the States."

Holly didn't know what else to ask him. "So, what are we doing here, Rick?"

"Waiting for Lance to phone from Langley," Rick said. "We assume he will, soon."

Rick's intercom buzzed and he picked up the phone. "Yes? Send him in."

Lance Cabot walked into the room and dropped a leather duffel and his briefcase on the carpet. "Morning, all." He flopped onto the sofa. "Now that we're all assembled, let's get down to it."

They waited for him to go on, but he didn't.

"Get down to what?" Holly asked, finally.

"This business with John, no middle initial, Simpson. Jean-Noël knew him—in fact, he brought him to Paris a while back."

"This is so," Ragot said.

"Tell us why," Lance said.

"Ron Spencer sent me and three others here to . . ." He stopped, looking doubtful.

"We're all family here," Lance said. "Tell us."

"To interrogate a Russian," Ragot said.

"At whose request?" Lance asked.

"Ron had a contact in the French national police who wanted the man spoken to."

"Don't the French police know how to conduct an interrogation?" Holly asked.

Ragot looked uncomfortable. "Of course, but our host didn't want this Russian to be known to his colleagues."

"Why did you choose Simpson to accompany you?" Lance asked.

"Simpson was something of an expert," Ragot said.

"In interrogation?" Rick asked.

"In . . . persuasion," Ragot replied. "Another of the team did the interrogation. Simpson was to persuade the subject to reply."

Everyone was silent for a moment before Lance spoke. "What was the identity of the Russian?"

"We never knew his name," Ragot asked.

"What was the name of Ron's friend in the police?"

"We never knew his name, either. Our instructions came from a man on the telephone. We never met him."

"What was the subject of the . . . conversation with the Russian gentleman?"

"The man apparently knew the identity of a spy for the Russians inside the Paris police."

"A spy for Russian intelligence?"

"I think not," Ragot said. "I formed the opinion that the spy was working not for Russian intelligence, but for other Russians, I know not who they were."

"Were you able to learn the name of the person who made the request from inside the Paris police?" Lance asked impatiently.

"No, we were not."

"I thought you said Simpson was expert at . . . persuasion."

"Oh, yes, Simpson did his job, all too well."

"I'm sorry?" Lance asked.

"The Russian expired before Simpson could persuade him to tell us the name—apparently of some preexisting condition of which we were not told."

"How long were Simpson's . . . attentions applied to the subject?"

"For about three hours. We came and went from time to time to check on his progress."

"If not the name of the informant, what else did you learn from the Russian gentleman?"

"Nothing, not even his name. He would not speak."

Nobody said anything for about a minute.

Holly broke the silence, and she was incredulous. "Simpson . . . *persuaded* the man for three hours and he revealed *nothing*?"

"I'm afraid that is correct."

"What happened after the interrogation ended?" Lance asked.

"I telephoned the number we had, the man answered, and we told him the subject had unexpectedly died. He asked if we had learned anything at all, and when I told him we had not he said that we should remove the body from Paris and dispose of it carefully. Then he hung up."

"That was it?" Lance asked.

"I telephoned the number again, and it was out of service."

"What did you do then?"

"Two of my colleagues and I returned to our hotel, Simpson having said that he would deal with the body. He returned late that night, and we all flew back to Berlin the following morning."

"And what did Simpson have to say about his efforts? Did he tell you where and how he disposed of the body?"

"Nothing. We never spoke of the incident again."

"Where did the interrogation take place?" Lance asked.

"In a garage in the twentieth arrondissement, near the Père-Lachaise cemetery. We arrived there to find the subject alone, bound and gagged. We never learned who brought him there or how."

"Well, it's all very neat, isn't it?" Lance said. He stood and picked up his bags. "I'm going to get some sleep," he said. "I'll be at the Plaza Athénée." Then he left.

"Well," Holly said, "that was bizarre."

Stone had just finished a room-service lunch when his cell phone rang. "Hello?"

"It's Ann," she said.

"How are you? How's the campaign?"

"I'm not sure about either of those."

"What's wrong?"

"I'm not sure about that, either. Everything seems fine, except Kate is dropping in the polls."

"Why?"

"We don't know for sure, but we suspect some sort of surreptitious campaign of lies. We just can't get a handle on it. Kate was up seven points in the polls and gained two more after the first debate, then the balloon started leaking air with each successive poll. We're down to a one-point lead, and with the margin of error at six percent, we're not even sure we're ahead."

"What are you doing about it?"

"We don't know what to do, except maintain a steady offense. I wish you were here."

"You don't need a lawyer, you need an operative who's just as sneaky as the opposition to figure this out."

"We're working on that. It's driving the press crazy, too, so they're working overtime to find out what's happening. The only good thing was the interview with the French deputy prime minister."

"The elegant Frenchwoman with the red hair?"

"That's the one."

"What was the interview?"

"She was being interviewed on Bloomberg TV, and she was asked what she thought of the economic policies of the Republican candidate, Hank Carson. When she answered the question, she referred to Carson as 'Honk.' Nobody heard anything after that, because we were all laughing so hard. Since then, everybody here, and some of the press, has been calling him 'Honk.' It's lifted our spirits a bit."

Stone laughed, too. "Somehow, it seems to fit him."

"Carson has tried so hard to get people to call him 'Hank,' to loosen his image, but hardly anybody has. Now everybody calls him 'Honk.'"

"And still, you're down in the polls?"

"We are. I wish I were in Paris with you. The press are at

me every minute, wanting to know what's wrong with our campaign, and I'm running out of brave faces to put on for them."

"Most races seem to tighten a bit in the last weeks, don't they?"

"Yes, but not this much. I mean, Kate is so clearly the superior candidate, I don't know why everybody hasn't gotten on her bandwagon. Hang on a minute." She covered the phone, and he could hear her voice, muffled. She seemed to be expressing consternation. Then she came back. "Mystery solved," she said, sounding dejected.

"Tell me."

"Some blogger named Howard Axelrod has concocted a story that a DNA test exists, proving that you are the father of Kate's baby."

Stone was immediately furious. "They tried that earlier, didn't they? It didn't hold water."

"He's saying that you've left the country because you don't want to be questioned about it. It's the rumor of the DNA test that's lending weight to the story."

"Well, if it's any consolation, I haven't donated any bodily tissues or fluids for purposes of DNA testing."

"Wait a minute," Ann said. "Have you had any sort of medical testing done in the past three months?"

"I had my biyearly flight physical, the one required by the FAA and my insurance company to keep me flying. That was about three weeks ago."

"Did they do blood work or take a urine sample?"

"Just the urine sample."

"That's enough for a DNA test, I think. Who's your doctor?"

"Samuel Somethingorother. I can't remember the last name. He's not my regular doctor, he's an AME—an Aviation Medical Examiner—appointed by the FAA. Actually, he's an ob-gyn who happens to be a pilot and thus has an interest in flying."

"I'll check him out. Let's hope to God he's not Kate's ob-gyn. What's his address?"

"He's in the East Seventies, up near the Carlyle Hotel."

"Oh, God, near Will and Kate's apartment."

Stone dug his FAA medical certificate from his wallet. "Wharton," he said. "Samuel C. Wharton, M.D."

"How were you referred to him?"

"There's a list of AMEs on an aviation website. I chose him because he was the closest to my house."

"Hang on a minute," Ann said, and covered the phone again.

Stone waited patiently.

Three minutes later, Ann came back on the line. "You're not going to believe this," she said.

"Try me."

"We looked him up on the Internet: Dr. Wharton and Kate were undergraduate classmates at Harvard."

"Is he her doctor?"

"I don't know. I don't even know if they knew each other in college, and I'm afraid to ask her."

"Well, *somebody* is going to have to ask her. There are too many coincidences here not to excite the interest of reporters."

"Stone, I hate to ask you this, but did you and Kate ever—"

"No! I've told you this before: Kate and I have never had any kind of physical relationship."

"I mean, I could understand it if you did—you're both such attractive people."

"Ann, stop it!"

"I'm so sorry, I'm just so worried."

"How about this: Kate and I take DNA tests on national television, from a doctor appointed by the Republican National Committee—"

"All right, all right! I'll stop it. I'll even ask Kate who her ob-gyn is!"

"I think you have to do that. Please let me know how this all turns out."

"You may start getting calls from reporters."

"I'll fend them off, get my calls screened—"

"No! That'll make you look guilty. Don't run from them, just answer the question."

"I hate doing that."

"I hate your having to do it. I'll call you when I've heard more." She hung up.

Five seconds after she did, Stone's phone buzzed. He checked the caller ID: Associated Press. He groaned.

27

S tone pressed the button. "Hello?"

"Stone Barrington?"

"Yes?"

"Is this Mr. Stone Barrington, an attorney at Woodman & Weld?"

"Yes, who's this?"

"Mr. Barrington, this is Jim Wardell, from the Associated Press."

"What can I do for you, Jim?"

"I'd just like to ask you a couple of questions."

"Shoot."

"Are you acquainted with a Dr. Samuel Wharton of New York?"

"I am."

"Have you ever seen him as a patient?"

"Yes, about three weeks ago."

"May I ask, did you have a medical complaint?"

"No, I had a need for a new medical certificate as a pilot."

"Did you say 'pilot'? As in an airplane?"

"Yes."

"Why did you need a new medical certificate?"

"Because my old one expires at the end of this month. All are required to have a medical exam every two years, in order to maintain their flying privileges. Airline pilots have to have one every six months."

"I see. Did you, as part of this medical exam, offer any bodily fluids for examination?"

"Well, I peed into a cup, if that's what you mean."

"Was this, ah, fluid sent to a lab for analysis?"

"I believe the way it's done is, you pee into the cup, the doctor dunks some sort of test strip in it, and if the strip turns the correct color, you're good, and they flush the rest."

"What color should it turn?"

"I've no idea. I think it's something to do with your blood sugar, and they want to know if you're diabetic. What's this about?"

"Do you know if Dr. Wharton is acquainted with Mrs. Katharine Lee?"

"Nope."

"Nope, she isn't?"

"Nope, I don't know if she is or isn't."

"Are you aware that Dr. Wharton is an ob-gyn?"

"Yes, I saw a certificate on his office wall."

"Then why were you seeing an ob-gyn for an aviation medical exam?"

"It's like this: the Federal Aviation Agency appoints doctors in every city as Aviation Medical Examiners, in order to ensure that pilots are healthy enough to fly safely. My former AME retired, so I needed a new one. I went to the AOPA website—"

"AO what?"

"The Aircraft Owners and Pilots Association."

"Right."

"They have a list of all the AMEs in various cities, and I picked Dr. Wharton because he was the nearest to my home."

"Did Katharine Lee recommend Dr. Wharton?"

"I just told you how I picked him. Are you having hearing problems?"

"No, I can hear you just fine."

"Then stop asking me questions I've already answered—it's annoying. Now I'm going to ask you just one more time: What's this call about? And if I don't get a straight answer, I'm hanging up."

"Mr. Barrington, are you aware of a contention from an Internet blogger named Howard Axelrod that you are the father of the baby that Mrs. Katharine Lee is carrying?"

"*What?* That's the stupidest thing I've ever heard!"

"Are you, sir?"

"Am I what? Did you say you're from the Associated Press?

Because I'm beginning to get the feeling you're from the Drudge Report."

"You didn't answer my question, Mr. Barrington."

"What question?"

"About the baby."

"Oh, that question. Let me spell it out for you: I am not the father of any baby that any woman on earth is carrying. Does that clear it up for you?"

"Does that include Katharine Lee's baby?"

"Didn't you hear me say 'any woman on earth'?"

"Yes, but—"

"But my ass, or rather, bite my ass. And don't call me again with stupid questions about something you came across on the Internet." Stone ended the call. Immediately, the phone rang again. He punched the button. "Hello?"

"Mr. Barrington, this is Joe Jerkison from the Drudge Report."

"Hi, there, got a pencil?"

"Yes, sir!"

"Then write this down: I, Stone Barrington, am not the father of any baby carried by any woman on earth. Got it?"

"Yes, sir, but—"

"Bye-bye." He hung up. The phone began ringing again. This time Stone found a paper clip, inserted it into the hole in the iPhone that opened the case, and disconnected the battery.

Peace!

Then the phone on his bedside table rang. Stone picked up the handset, punched line two, and called the operator.

"How may I help you, Mr. Barrington?"

"I'd like the operator to screen all my calls before putting them through."

"Yes, sir."

"Here is a list of names of people from whom I will accept calls." He rattled off a dozen names. "Anyone else who calls is to be told that I am not available and that it is not known when or if I will be available. Is that clear?"

"And what if the person calling insists on speaking to you?"

"Then hang up."

"Yes, sir. For how long shall your calls be screened?"

"Until I check out of the hotel."

"Yes, sir."

Stone hung up.

S tone replaced the battery in his iPhone and rere-
corded his answering message to reflect the statement he had given to the AP and the Drudge guy,
then he called his office. Busy signal. He reflected on the fact
that he had four lines, then he called the cell number of his
secretary, Joan.

"Hello, goddammit."

"Joan?"

"Stone, is that you?"

"It is. Did you confuse me with our Maker?"

"I'm sorry, but the phones have gone nuts here."

"Same here. Get your steno pad." She did, and he dictated

his statement. "Put that in as the recording on our answering system, then stop answering the phones, until they stop ringing."

"That doesn't make any sense."

"You know what I mean. Have I had any calls from people I actually know?"

"Who knows? I stopped answering half an hour ago."

"It doesn't matter. I don't want to hear from anyone who doesn't have my cell number. Do you have any idea how the Associated Press and the Drudge Report got my cell number?"

"Those people have ways of getting anybody's number."

"Well, don't tell anyone I'm in Paris, or they'll start knocking on my door here." Someone started knocking on the door to his suite, then it got louder. "I'm here, if you need me," Stone said, then hung up and went to the door.

He checked the peephole and found Holly waiting. "Who is it?"

"Eet ees zee sexual crimes deeveesion of zee Paree gendarmes!"

Stone opened the door. "In that case, come right in."

Holly came in. "Sorry, I forgot my key card. What's going on? You look a little frazzled."

Stone closed the door. "I'm being pursued by multiple members of the media."

"Maddening!"

"You bet your sweet ass. Some blogger jerk named Howard Axelrod has blogged that Kate Lee is carrying my baby."

"Well, congratulations to both of you! And to her husband, too, for being so broad-minded."

"Stop it, you know it isn't true. Or even possible."

"I know no such thing," Holly replied, "and given your nature, it's certainly possible."

"I've never even been alone with Kate."

"I believe the standard line is 'We are just good friends.'"

"Yeah, I'll try that on the next reporter who calls."

"You know," Holly said, "for someone who is being pursued by multiple members of the media, your phones are oddly silent."

"I've had the hotel screen my calls, and—so far, at least— only two of the multiple members of the media have learned my cell number."

"You know who Howard Axelrod is, don't you?"

"I do not."

"That's okay, neither does anybody else. People have been trying to track him down for months."

"Why?"

"Because he keeps reporting breaking news before anybody else. I expect Matt Drudge is contemplating suicide by now. The bad news is, Mr. Axelrod is always right."

"Not anymore, he isn't."

"I believe that makes you the exception that proves the rule."

"That line has never made any sense."

"Every schoolteacher I've ever had has spouted it."

Stone's cell phone rang. He looked at the caller ID and found two lines drawn across the screen and showed it to Holly. "Should I answer it?"

"Sure, and put it on speaker—I could use some entertainment."

Stone pressed the button. "Yes?"

"It's me," Lance drawled.

"I'm sorry, you'll have to be more specific."

"Stone, I've just had some wonderful news: Kate Lee is carrying your baby!"

Holly broke up.

"I'm so happy for both of you," Lance said.

"Go fuck yourself, Lance."

"As much fun as that might be, I'd like to speak to Holly instead. Don't bother telling me she's not there—I can hear her chortling."

Holly took the phone from Stone. "I don't chortle, Lance, I chuckle."

"Ah, there you are, Holly. Have you and your two colleagues come up with any decisive information in the matter of John, no middle initial, Simpson?"

"We have not."

"You haven't learned how he disposed of the body of the Russian gentleman?"

"We have not. We have no usable information."

"That is not quite correct," Lance said. "We know that the Russian combine has a spy inside the Paris police."

"Well, we know that someone inside the Paris police believes that strongly enough to have someone tortured to learn the alleged spy's identity."

"It offends me that that person has used my personnel to try and solve his own problem," Lance said. "It's time we put a stop to that sort of thing."

"And how do we do that?" Holly asked.

"We don't, really—Stone does."

"Stone does what?" Stone asked.

"Stone calls his *petit bijou*, Mirabelle, and tells her that her father might like to know that there's a Russian combine spy in his prefecture."

"I don't think that's a very good idea," Stone said.

"Why not?"

"Her father appears to have a low opinion of Americans, in general, and those connected to the CIA, in particular. He considers me an American spy and is unlikely to attach any credence to any information originating from me."

"Then how about her brother?"

"What about her brother?"

"Would you seem a more credible source to him?"

"I've met him only once, and in a circumstance unlikely to add to my credibility."

"Still, in the past Jacques has been able to set personal considerations aside, when it is in his interests to do so."

"Surely there is a better way to communicate with Jacques Chance than through his sister."

"If there were a better way, Stone, I would have thought of it. Come along, now, it's time to do something for your country."

Stone sighed. "Oh, all right. What do you want me to tell her?"

"Everything you know would do nicely."

"I don't know all that much."

"Just so. Tell her that. Bye-bye." Lance hung up.

"How did I get mixed up in all this?" Stone said to Holly.

"By fucking the daughter and sister of highly placed French policemen?" Holly suggested.

Stone couldn't argue with that.

tone picked up the phone. "Now listen," he said to Holly, "you have to keep your mouth shut while I'm on the phone with Mirabelle, do you understand?"

"Not a word," Holly said.

Stone chose Mirabelle's number from his list of Favorites, and it began ringing. Finally she picked up. "Ah, it's the American spy!" she said. "To what do I owe this invasion?"

"I'm sorry if I'm invading," Stone said, "but I have to talk with you about your brother."

"What could you possibly say to me about my brother? You don't even know him."

"Let's just say that I know people who know him—and

respect him—and I have some information for him that he might find very interesting."

"And you want me to give him this information?"

"If you could pass it along, I'm sure he and I would both be very grateful."

"Is this police business?"

"Sort of, I guess."

"Then it would be better if a policeman spoke to him. He has contempt for people who are not policemen."

"That's a very large group of people," Stone said.

"Nevertheless."

"Nevertheless what?"

"Nevertheless, he has contempt for non-policemen."

"Tell you what: if we can arrange a meeting, I will supply a bona fide policeman with whom he can speak, while ignoring all non-policemen."

"I am having a drink with him at six o'clock this evening. You may join us at a lovely sidewalk café near the Boulevard Saint-Germain."

"I'm afraid that the security arrangements that have been made for me preclude exposing my person to the evening air. How about if you both come to l'Arrington for a drink in my suite, at six o'clock."

"Who will be there?"

"A policeman and, if he wishes, a member of our intelligence services."

"All right, I will arrange it. Be sure to have pastis—that is all he drinks. *Au revoir.*" She hung up.

148

"Were you referring to me?" Holly asked.

"I was."

"Oh, good. I want to get a good look at her."

"Holly . . ."

"Didn't I behave myself while you were on the phone with her?"

"Well, yes . . ."

"I will behave myself while in the same room with her, as well."

"All right," he said, "but I will unceremoniously throw you out if you let your worse nature get the better of you."

"Fair enough. And, by the way, don't you think you'd better inform the policeman in question that his services are required?"

"Right you are." Stone called Dino.

"Hey."

"Where are you?"

"Exiting a dull meeting."

"Can you be here at six—you and Viv—for a drink with a Paris cop?"

"Sure, I guess. Who is he?"

"One Jacques Chance."

"I shook his hand yesterday."

"Good, that will help. Be here at a quarter to six. I have to brief you on what to say."

"What do I have to say?"

"I'll tell you at a quarter to six."

"Okay."

Stone hung up, called room service and asked for a bottle of pastis.

"What is pastis?" Holly asked.

"Some sort of French booze. It's all Chance drinks, apparently."

The waiter arrived in record time, clutching a bottle.

Stone invited him in. "How do I prepare a drink with this?"

"You just add cool water," the man said. "Four or five to one of the pastis."

"Got it."

"Or you might offer your guests a small pitcher—such as the one in your bar—filled with water, and let them decide how much."

Stone slipped the man a fifty-euro note. "I'm grateful to you," he said. The man left, very happy.

Holly opened the bottle and took a small swig, then screwed up her face. "Holy shit!"

"He said to mix it with four or five parts of water."

"I didn't hear that part."

"That's what you get for drinking from the bottle."

"It's how I was brought up," she said.

30

Dino and Viv let themselves into the sitting room from their adjoining bedroom on time, and Stone sat them down and gave them a drink while he briefed Dino on what to say.

"Got it," Dino said, sounding bored.

"Why does Dino have to do this, instead of you?" Viv asked.

"Because Chance, to put it in the words of his sister, 'has contempt for non-policemen.'"

"That's a little stiff, isn't it?"

"Nevertheless," Stone said, quoting Mirabelle further.

At precisely six o'clock there was a sharp rap on the door; Stone answered it and ushered in his guests. "M'sieur Prefect," he said, "may I present the police commissioner of the city of New York, Dino Bacchetti? Commissioner, this is Prefect Jacques Chance, of the Paris police."

"We met yesterday," Chance said, with a small smile as he shook Dino's hand.

"May I also present Vivian Bacchetti, the commissioner's wife, and also Madame Holly Barker, who is an important official of my country's Central Intelligence Agency."

"*Enchanté*," Chance said, lightly kissing the hands of both women.

"Charmed, I'm sure," Holly said drily.

Stone gestured toward Mirabelle. "And this is the prefect's sister, Madame Mirabelle Chance, the famous Parisian couturier." Dino, to Stone's astonishment, kissed her hand.

Everyone took a seat.

"May I offer you a pastis, M'sieur Prefect?" Stone asked.

"You may," Chance said.

"And Mirabelle?"

"Vodka martini, straight up, two olives stuffed with anchovies," Mirabelle replied. "If you please." Mirabelle well knew the contents of Stone's bar.

Stone quickly mixed the martini, then poured a substantial pastis and offered both drinks on a tray, along with a small silver pitcher of water, containing one ice cube. They accepted the drinks, and the prefect added a judicious amount of water from the pitcher.

"I was very impressed with your presentation earlier this week, Commissioner," Chance said. "You gave me some ideas for my own jurisdiction."

"Thank you, Prefect," Dino said. "Tell me, being an American, I am uncertain of the difference between your office and that of your father."

"My father, Michel, is prefect of the national police, of the whole country. I am prefect of the police of the city of Paris, plus three other adjoining departments, much as your own jurisdiction includes Manhattan, plus four other boroughs," Chance explained.

Mirabelle spoke up. "Jacques likes to think that his job is by far the more difficult and important of the two jurisdictions."

The prefect managed a slightly haughty laugh. "It is my sister, not I, who has . . . How do you put it? Delusions of grandeur?"

Everyone chuckled appreciatively.

"Now," Chance said, "I have been informed that you, Commissioner, have some information of interest to me to convey."

"Yes, Prefect," Dino said. "But first, having heard that you enjoy the company of other policemen, I should tell you that Madame Bacchetti is a retired detective first grade of the NYPD, and that Madame Barker, before joining her present employer, was a military police officer of the United States Army and the chief of police of a significant city in our state of Florida."

"I am very impressed, Commissioner," Chance said. "How is it that M'sieur Barrington comes to be in such distinguished company?"

"My friend Stone is a veteran of fourteen years of the NYPD," Dino said, "ten of them as a detective and my partner during those years. He also held the rank of detective first grade."

"Ah," Chance said, "so we are all colleagues here."

"Except me," Mirabelle said, a little too sweetly.

"Yours is a more intriguing profession," Holly said to her, "and I'm sure you come by more intelligence each day than I do in my job."

Everyone chuckled appreciatively.

"Now," Dino said, "may I call you Jacques?"

"Oh, please."

"And I am Dino to my colleagues. Now, Jacques, it has come to my attention, through Madame Barker's intelligence service, that there appears to be a highly placed person in your prefecture who is also employed by a Russian criminal organization, and who reports to them on the activities of your prefecture on a regular basis."

Chance's expression remained frozen, except that his eyebrows shot up. "If your information is correct," he said, "then it is most distressing to me. How, may I ask," he said, turning toward Holly, "did your agency come by this knowledge?"

"We learned that a four-man team of professionals were hired to interrogate a member of the Russian organization, in order to learn the name of the person in your prefecture."

"Ah! And what is the name, according to the interrogatee?"

"I'm afraid that the interrogatee, who, unknown to his interrogators, had a serious medical condition, died before he could reveal the name, in spite of having been questioned under stressful conditions for three hours. He refused to speak at all."

Chance threw up his hands. "Well," he said, "that is most disappointing. Perhaps if his interrogators had come to me I might have been able to help in the interrogation, without actually killing the interrogatee."

"It was unfortunate," Holly said, "but beyond the scope of my agency. We learned of the situation only after the fact, from a confidential informant."

"Perhaps, if I could speak to your informant?"

"I'm told that he has left France, and his name is unknown to me."

Dino spoke up. "I should say that, in spite of the disappointing nature of this information, it has revealed, to the satisfaction of the Agency, that this spy in your prefecture exists, and that is important intelligence in itself."

"Important, but frustrating," Chance said. "Tell me, was this Agency able to learn any details of this spy, other than he is, as you say, 'highly placed'?"

"Regrettably," Holly said, "we have no other information about him, but we thought it important, as well as a necessary professional courtesy, to tell you what we had learned."

"Of course, I appreciate your professional courtesy," Chance said, "and I would be most grateful if you would continue to pass along any further information that you might acquire in the future."

"Certainly, we will," Holly said. "However, all of us in this room will be leaving France quite soon, so I will ask our Paris station chief, Richard LaRose, whom I understand you know, to communicate directly with you should he come into new information."

Chance looked at his watch. "If you will excuse me," he said, rising, "I have another engagement." He turned to Mirabelle, who was showing no signs of moving. "And so do you," he said pointedly.

Reluctantly, Mirabelle got to her feet. Goodbyes were said, hands were kissed, and Prefect Chance and his sister made their exit.

"Well," Holly said after they had gone, "she was really quite interesting, wasn't she?"

As they were finishing their drinks, Holly's cell phone rang, and she answered it. "Yes? Hi." She listened for a moment, then covered the phone. "Lance is on the phone. He wants us to have dinner with him."

"Do we have to?" Stone asked.

"He says he has more information about Simpson."

"Dino? Viv?"

They both shrugged and nodded.

"Okay, where?"

Holly asked the question and was answered. "At Le Restaurant de L'Hôtel," she said. "Thirteen Rue des Beaux-Arts."

"At the restaurant at the hotel?" Stone asked. "Sounds pretty generic."

"L'Hôtel is the hotel where Oscar Wilde died, Lance said. I suppose Le Restaurant is their restaurant. He's on his way there now."

Stone summoned the van, and they went downstairs. "I've begun to think of this thing as my hearse," he said, as they boarded. Ten minutes later they drew to a halt in a narrow street, and waited while the two men up front cased the block and pronounced it safe.

They entered the hotel, where someone at the front desk told them to proceed straight ahead. They passed through a comfortable bar and emerged into a small but lushly decorated dining room. Lance sat at a table in the rear of the room, and he waved them over. Stone noted that, in contrast to his appearance that morning, he was now freshly groomed and wearing a beautifully tailored suit. Lance seated the party so that the women were on either side of him, and he ordered their drinks from memory.

"I thought you would like to know that there is a restaurant in Paris that stocks Knob Creek," he said to Stone.

"I'm relieved to hear it," Stone replied. "I managed to force the bar at l'Arrington to serve it, but it's scarce on the ground in this town."

Their drinks arrived and they were given menus. "It's a short menu," Lance said, "but everything on it is good. They have a star from Michelin, and I'm sure they'd have another, if they could expand the *carte*.

"How did your meeting with M'sieur Chance go?" Lance asked after they had ordered.

"It was brief," Stone said, wondering how Lance knew of the meeting. "I had been told that Chance detests people who aren't policemen, so I asked Dino to give him what news we had."

"And his reaction?"

"Annoyance that we didn't give him more," Stone said. "He as much as said that, if he had been conducting the interrogation of the Russian, we would now know everything."

"Who's to say he's wrong?" Lance asked.

"I was told you now have more information about John, no middle initial, Simpson."

"I do," Lance said, "by the simple expedient of releasing his service record to myself. Unfortunately, because of its restricted reading list, I can't show it to any of you, but I can tell you what's in it—there's no restriction on that, as long as the recipients of the information are properly cleared, and I have the power to clear you all, just like *that!*" He snapped his fingers, then made the sign of the cross. "You are, as of this moment, all cleared, my children. Your clearance expires when the bill for dinner arrives, and you must never reveal anything I have told you, on pain of a polite refusal at the gates of heaven."

"Why don't you just give us the high points, Lance?" Stone asked.

"I'm afraid there aren't any high points, Stone, only low ones. It seems that 'Simps,' as he was called by those who pretended to be his friends, lived his life moving from one low point to another. I am ashamed that such people are an absolute necessity if one expects to operate an effective intelligence service."

"I'll take your word for it," Stone said.

"Can you summarize, Lance?" Holly asked.

"Well, let's see: he was, as you know, brought to our attention by Our Man in Afghanistan, who had seen him maim and kill his way through the various mountain passes and villages, then sit down at dinner and eat two steaks. He arrived at the Farm for training having already learned just about everything one needs to know about killing another. He was especially adept at the use of almost any sort of blade. One of his trainers said that with a couple of weeks' training, he could have won Olympic Gold with the épée. That amounts to high praise from such a figure."

"Not the guy you'd want to meet in a dark alley," Dino said.

"Not the guy you'd want to meet anywhere," Lance said. "In the army, he fired expert with every weapon they handed him, and at the Farm, he amazed his tutors by hitting everything he saw from the hip—no actual aiming of a weapon. As they got to evaluate him and know him better they found they had discovered a man, not only with no conscience but with no scruples or, for that matter, pity, either. One instructor entered the following in his training record: 'He is the kind of man to whom you could say, go kill these three people and report back in a week, and he'd be home for supper, wiping the blood off his hands.'"

"Jesus," Holly said.

"Quite. And when you think of the sort of people who wrote these evaluations, who are not easily impressed by the capacity for mayhem of others, it all becomes especially chilling. Every fitness report written by everyone he ever reported to makes note of, as one supervising officer put it, 'not his courage, but more his absolute lack of fear of anything or anybody.' The two things are very different—the latter, I think, tends to be psychotic."

Dinner arrived, and they approached their food more gingerly than they might have before Lance's report. While they waited for dessert, Lance continued.

"So, I think we all see the kind of man Simps was, and we can all be happy that he is in a pauper's grave in some French cemetery. It is astonishing to me that he met his end in the kitchen of a cottage, at the hands of a small woman with a very old shotgun. If my Agency had a medal that covered those circumstances, I would award it to her without hesitation."

"Lance," Stone said, "do you now have any idea what Simpson was doing there?"

"Well, it seems obvious that he went there to kill at least one, perhaps both of the other people present in the cottage that night. Certainly, if he had killed one, and the other had witnessed it, he would have had no hesitation in making the score two–love." Lance paused and took a deep breath. "Unless, of course, he had been instructed not, under any circumstances, to kill the other. Do you see where this is leading us?"

"Wait a minute," Holly said, "was Simpson freelancing for anyone who'd pay his price? Is that what you're saying?"

"I think," Lance said, "that it is impossible not to come to that conclusion, and, apparently, he had been freelancing for some time. Simpson had a bank balance, back in Virginia, of more than two hundred thousand dollars, and he didn't earn it on a civil servant's salary. It also seems that, after the death of the unfortunate Russian gentleman at Simps's hands, he had all the time in the world to report to the man who hired him, before he rejoined his colleagues at their hotel. He had been to Paris three times on earlier occasions that we know about, so he had every opportunity of meeting and being hired by someone there."

Stone spoke up. "Let's get back to where all this is leading us. What are your conclusions?"

Lance spread his hands. "I conclude, from the available evidence—which would not convict anyone in any honest court—that Simpson was hired to kill you, Stone, not the sister of the man who hired him."

Stone stared at Lance, unbelieving. "Lance, are you saying that Jacques Chance hired Simpson to kill *me*?"

"After what I've told you," Lance said, "can you come to any other conclusion? He certainly didn't hire the man to kill his sister, whom he loves deeply and, gossip has it, perhaps too much."

Holly perked up. "I want to hear about that part, please."

"Chance has a history, going back to his late teens—around the time that Mirabelle achieved puberty—of an extreme overprotectiveness toward his sister, and of dealing harshly with any male who had even the least of designs on her. A highly qualified psychiatrist I spoke to told me that his behavior is indicative of an obsession with his female sibling, though that doesn't mean that he ever did anything about it. By the way, Jacques has never married, nor has he ever exhibited an interest in another woman, except for the most immediate sorts of gratification, not all of them affectionate. Since her teens he has lavished affection on Mirabelle, giving her expensive gifts, escorting her to public events, and backing her financially in her business—in short, the sort of attention that most Frenchmen bestow on a mistress, rather less on a wife."

Dino raised a finger. "So, Jacques wants Stone killed because he sees him as a threat to his relationship with his sister?"

"How beautifully you cut to the chase, Dino," Lance said, flicking a bread crumb off his cuff with his napkin. "There is another possible motive, though: Jacques Chance is very likely the person who you have just told him is giving information on police operations to a Russian mob. He very probably hired the freelance team from the Berlin station to interrogate a member of that mob, to see if he would be exposed. Once the interrogatee died without having exposed him, Jacques felt more comfortable in his position as a spy. Until Stone came along."

"Why would he see me as a threat to his position?" Stone asked.

"Because Jacques shares his father's loathing of American intelligence operatives, and he has grossly overrated your importance in that regard."

"So you have two motives," Dino pointed out. "Which do you favor?"

"Both, actually," Lance said. "They are not mutually exclusive, and taken together, they at least double his resolve to remove Stone from the scene. I expect there may even be a synergistic effect."

"Sounds as though I should get out of town," Stone said.

"I'm afraid that wouldn't help, Stone. My psychiatric colleague believes that Jacques is now so fixated upon your removal from the corporeal plane that he would likely pursue you to the proverbial ends of the earth."

"Lance," Stone said, "do you have a resolution to this situation in mind, or should I just offer myself up for sacrifice?"

"Well, the easy way out would be just to make Jacques disappear—ironically the sort of job for which Mr. Simpson would have been so well suited. That sort of action, however, is fraught with peril—legal, political, congressional, et cetera, et cetera. I think a better course might be to simply expose the prefect for what he is: a hater of his father and the authority over him that the old man represents. That, incidentally, is his motive for selling out to the Russians."

"And how would that be accomplished?" Stone asked.

"I had at first thought that a word in the shell-like ear of a well-placed French journalist might do, but the libel laws in Europe are so much more difficult to deal with than back home, and of course, there would be the fear of personal retaliation from Jacques, who is fully capable of that."

"So?"

"I think the answer might lie with the peculiar gifts of one Howard Axelrod."

Stone made a groaning noise.

"There, there, Stone," Lance said, reaching over and patting his hand, "I know your experience with Mr. Axelrod—that is not his real name, of course—has not been favorable, but you are, unfortunately, living evidence of the power the man wields. A couple of days ago you were a semi-anonymous New York lawyer. Now half the world believes you to be the sire of the child now carried by the putative Next President of the United States. Need I say more?"

"You need not," Stone admitted.

Holly leaned in. "What is Howard Axelrod's real name, Lance?"

"Now, now, Holly, if that were revealed, then I would not have the leverage with Mr. Axelrod that I need to ensure his cooperation in this noble effort."

"You have a point," Holly admitted. "But later, I'm going to make you tell me."

"Certainly exposing Howard Axelrod for who he is would be great fun," Lance said, "but not until I have persuaded him to expose Jacques Chance for who he is. Which brings me to a point: Stone, between the time the first story about Jacques begins to circulate, and the time at which the facts have made him harmless to you, there lies a period of as yet undetermined length when Jacques will be made more dangerous than ever to your continued existence. There will come a moment, though, when it will be propitious for you to flee Paris and Europe. I will get word to you when that moment arrives. In the meantime, however, do not travel except in the coach and six provided for you, and make arrangements for an instantaneous departure when the word comes."

"You bet your ass," Stone said with conviction.

"One thing, Lance," Holly said.

"Yes, Holly?"

"Do not spring Stone from Paris until *after* the grand opening of l'Arrington."

"Why not?"

"Because Stone is taking me, and I have spent a month's salary on a gown for the occasion. If Stone vanishes, then I will *get* you."

Lance laughed uproariously. "And that would be a fate worse than Stone's at the hands of Jacques Chance! All right, Holly, I'll see that you get to wear your gown."

S tone got into bed, exhausted, longing for sleep.
Holly, on the other hand, was brightly awake,
sitting up in bed with a book on her lap. She was
not reading it. "Stone!" she exploded.

"Mmmf? What is it?"

"Who do you think Howard Axelrod really is?"

Stone turned over, presenting his back to her. "I haven't the
faintest idea."

"Surely you must be curious. He's supposed to be a well-
known journalist."

"I'm not curious, I'm tired." Stone pulled the covers half
over his head.

"Well, it's somebody with a bit of wit, anyway. He always makes me laugh. Somehow, I think he'd like me, too."

"I hope the two of you will be very happy." Stone turned onto his back. Then he lifted his head. "Wait a minute," he said, "you're talking about the son of a bitch who has besmirched my good name and called Kate's character into question?"

"Your name wasn't all that good before, not with regard to women, anyway, and Kate's character is beyond reproach. This will pass in a day or two, wait and see."

"I don't have a choice, do I?"

"I think Howard Axelrod is in Paris," Holly said.

That got Stone's attention. "Why do you think that?"

"Well, Lance is awfully sure of his ability to manipulate Axelrod, and that would be easier to do if they're both in the same city."

"Well, if you find out who and where he is, let me know— I'd like to take a swing at the bastard, and no judge would punish me for it."

"The gathering of top policemen has drawn top journalists from everywhere to Paris. I'll bet Howard is among them."

"I haven't heard anything about that."

"It was in this morning's *International New York Times*."

"I didn't see it."

"Would you really take a swing at him?"

"You bet your sweet ass I would." Stone was wide awake now.

"Do you really think Mirabelle Chance has been sleeping with her brother all these years?"

"I confess, that came as something of a shock to me when Lance brought it up. I think it's a horribly damaging rumor, and I don't believe for a moment that she has that in her character."

"I rather liked her this evening. She seemed like a no-bullshit sort of person, very forthright. What is she like in bed? Is she enthusiastic, or does she just lie back and think of France?"

"Holly, shut up and go to sleep."

"I mean, I'm the only woman I know anything about in bed—other women are a mystery to me."

"They're a mystery to me, too," Stone said. "I mean, you're in bed with me right now, and you're talking about how other women perform sex. That is a *complete* mystery to me."

"Don't you ever wonder how other men perform in bed?"

"I have never wondered for a moment, and I don't care."

"You have no sexual curiosity, Stone."

"Not about that, I don't. You leave women to me, and I'll leave other men to you."

"Don't you care if I fuck other men?"

"It's none of my business, is it? Have I ever said a word to you on that subject?"

"I suppose not. Would you like to hear about some of them?"

"I would not!"

"Well, there was this one guy—I think you might know him—"

"Stop it! Not another word!"

"I wonder what Howard Axelrod is like in the sack."

"Incapable, I should think, given his deep interest in other people's sex lives."

"Stone, everybody is interested in other people's sex lives."

"Not I."

"Why do you think people go to hot movies and read hot novels? They're dying to know how other people do it, that's why."

"I don't read hot novels, and I hardly ever go to the movies, for any reason. I see movies on television, old and new, and TV, the networks, at least, haven't gotten around to explicit sex, yet."

"It's only a matter of time. Cable and satellite are already way ahead of the networks in that regard. I'll bet l'Arrington has half a dozen X-rated channels on its television system right now. Where's the remote control?" She rummaged around under the covers until she came to Stone. She laid a hand on his crotch. "Are you still sleepy?" she breathed into his ear.

"Not very," he replied.

"Oh, good. Let's make our own X-rated movie." She brought him erect.

He rolled over on top of her. "No pictures, please."

"Just memories," she said, guiding him in.

At ten A.M. the phone at Stone's bedside rang; Stone turned over and answered before it occurred to him that he had ordered all his calls screened. "Hello?"

"Sleeping in?" Lance asked.

"I was."

"Put Holly on the extension. I need to speak with you both."

"Hang on." Stone poked Holly's sleeping ass with a finger, then, getting no response, poked it harder.

"What?" she said into her pillow.

"It's Lance. He wants to speak to both of us."

Holly rolled over and picked up the phone on her side. "What, Lance?"

"Now don't be grumpy, this is an important call."

"I can't wait to hear it," she said.

"There is an exciting event this evening—a dinner for a couple dozen of America's top journalists, and you and Stone are invited, if you don't have other plans. If you do have other plans, kindly rearrange them."

"We don't have plans, do we, Stone?"

Stone shook his head.

"We're available. Now can we go back to sleep?"

"Of course, my dear. Seven-thirty for eight at the United States ambassador's residence. See you then!" Lance hung up.

"Did he say the ambassador's residence?" Stone asked.

"I believe he did."

"Been there, done that—don't want to do it again."

"I'm afraid we've already accepted, and it does sound exciting. I never get to meet journalists in my job. I wonder why Lance wants me there?"

"I don't know, but I'll go only if you stand between me and the ambassador at all times."

"Didn't you enjoy being felt up by the lady last time?"

"No, I did not. I want your solemn word."

"Oh, all right, you have it. It's a good thing you're not a woman, you know."

"Why is that?"

"Because women get groped all the time."

"They do? I wasn't aware of that."

"That's because you're doing the groping. If you were the gropee, you'd be shocked."

"I don't grope unless invited."

"You mean women walk up to you at dinner parties and say, 'Grope me'?"

"Not exactly—it's more subtle than that."

"Enlighten me."

"Well, do you remember the party at Dino's apartment, when you backed into me and wiggled your ass against me? Like that."

"Oh, my goodness, I did do that, didn't I?"

"Yes, and it was an invitation to be groped."

"And it worked, too!" She put her hand under the covers and drew her nails across his bare ass. "Consider that an invitation," she said. "R.S.V.P.?"

STONE SAW TO IT that they arrived at the ambassador's residence just a little late; he wanted a lot of people there when the ambassador greeted them, and his plan worked.

"Stone! Holly!" the ambassador crowed. "How nice to see you again."

Stone reached around Holly and shook her hand. "Ambassador, you look lovely this evening." She was wearing a clinging red dress that showed off her well-toned body.

"Why, thank you!"

Lance materialized beside her, and before Stone could warn him he saw the ambassador's hand head for its target. Lance started only a bit. "Come," he said, "there are people to meet."

He took Holly by the hand and led her away; Stone followed, firmly attached to her other hand.

In short order, they were introduced to Walter Grimes, a columnist for the *Washington Post*; Charles Danforth, an editor of the *Boston Globe*; Helen Frank, the *NBC Nightly News* anchorwoman; Carla Fontana, the Washington bureau chief for the *New York Times*; Paul Roberts, the editor of the *International New York Times*; Tim Bartlett, the Paris correspondent for the Associated Press; and Rod Halliburton, the White House correspondent for Politico.

Holly was dazzled. "It's so interesting to put faces to all these names," she said. Lance towed them around the room, adding another dozen names and faces to the introductions. He seemed to be an old friend of each of them.

Helen Frank sidled up to Stone at the first opportunity. "Are you *the* Stone Barrington?" she asked.

"The *only* one, as far as I know," Stone replied cordially.

"The, ah, *friend* of Katharine Lee?"

"The just good friend of same. I've already released a statement to that effect, and I have nothing to add."

"How disappointing, I was hoping for a scoop," she said, feigning petulance.

"Nothing exists to be scooped, I'm afraid."

"Tell me," she said, leaning in close. "Has the ambassador made a move on your crotch this evening? I've heard rumors."

"Not this evening," Stone said. "Holly, here, is running interference."

"And what a lovely interference she is," the woman said, drifting away.

Holly pulled Lance a step away from the others. "Is he here?"

"Is who here?" Lance asked innocently.

"Howard Axelrod."

"Oh, yes, he is present, and we've already had our little chat."

"Introduce me."

"You may have already met him," Lance said, then the ambassador pulled him away to meet someone else.

Shortly, they were called to dinner in a room full of tables of six, and Holly spent the rest of the evening speculating on which of the guests was the dreaded Howard Axelrod.

As the party broke up, Stone encountered Lance, lingering with a group. "May we offer you a lift?" he asked.

"Thank you, no," Lance replied. "I'm staying for a little while to have a brandy with the ambassador."

"Watch yourself," Stone said.

"I intend to," Lance said with his little smile.

"What was that brief conversation with Lance about?" Holly asked, when they were safely in the van.

"I'm not sure," Stone replied, "but Lance is either very innocent or very knowing—I'm not sure which."

"Probably both," Holly said.

The van hummed along for a while then made a turn, heading for a bridge over the Seine. "Oh, God," Stone said, rubbing his face vigorously.

"What's wrong?" Holly asked.

"I'm having a very intense *déjà vu*," he said.

"What's it about?"

"I'm driving along like this, Lance and Rick and me, and as we enter this intersection ahead, we're broadsided by a concrete-mixer truck. That actually happened last year, and I'm reliving it."

"Do you survive?" Holly said.

"Of course, I'm here, right?"

"It could never happen twice," she said.

They stopped for a traffic light. Stone was perspiring and wiping his face with a handkerchief.

"You don't look well," Holly said.

"I'll be all right when we're across the bridge."

The light changed, and they entered the intersection with the other traffic and headed for the bridge. Stone quickly looked both ways.

"All clear," Holly said. "I checked, and we're safe on the bridge."

"Thank God," Stone said. "I thought I was going to throw up."

The van left the Pont Royal and started across the wide intersection where the Quai Voltaire met the Quai Anatole France. Stone heard an engine revving, and he looked up to see a large mass emblazoned with the name "Aveco" rushing at the van. Then there was an incredibly loud noise and his world turned upside down, then right-side up again, and the van was sliding sideways toward the parapet between the street and the Seine while the vehicle seemed to be peppered with silent fire. The truck was still revving, and the now upright van traveled across the sidewalk, struck the parapet, breaking it, and when it finally came to rest, Stone was staring forward through the windshield into the River Seine, perhaps twenty feet below.

Holly had been thrown onto the van's floor, and she struggled back to her feet with a Glock in her hand. "So much for *déjà vu!*" she shouted. "Let's get out of here!"

"No!" came a shout from the driver. "If you get out we'll go into the river!"

"Then you get out first!" Holly shouted back. "And be quick about it!"

The two men up front struggled with their doors. "They're jammed!" one of them yelled.

"Then come back here!" Stone shouted.

The two men climbed uphill into the passenger compartment and Stone began yanking on the sliding door. "Need some help, here!"

One of the men started kicking the door, and it flew open. The four of them spilled out of the van into a sea of gravel, on the opposite side from the well-aimed truck. Three of them had weapons in their hands and were pointing them in all directions. There was the sound of running boots striking the pavement, away from them, then the sound of approaching sirens. All this seemed to Stone to have happened in seconds.

"Let's get out of here," the driver said, sticking his submachine gun under his coat. "I don't want to have to explain this to the police."

"Which way?" Holly asked.

"Back across the bridge, away from this mess. Don't run, walk. Try not to attract attention."

"Maybe you should return the Glock to wherever it came from," Stone suggested.

Holly shoved it back into her handbag but kept looking around for hostiles. They hurried across the bridge as a group, looking in all directions, while the driver muttered into a handheld radio. He took it away from his lips for a moment.

"Check yourselves. Anybody hurt? Any blood? Any broken limbs?"

"All right here," Holly said, and Stone said the same.

"We've got a car five minutes out," the driver said. "Let's stand behind that bus shelter." They crossed the Quai des Tuileries and huddled behind the shelter.

"What's happening across the river?" Holly asked. "I can't see a thing."

"It was a big dump truck loaded with gravel. That was the noise like bullets striking the van—there's gravel everywhere."

"What the hell would a dump truck be doing out at this time of night?" Holly asked.

"Looking for us," Stone said. "Or rather, for me."

"Did anybody see the driver?"

"I saw a man running," the driver's companion said. "Big guy, black or dark clothes, heavy boots."

"Like the French assault-team cops wear?" Stone asked.

"Exactly like that," the man said.

They continued to huddle behind the bus shelter, waiting for rescue. Holly had the Glock in her hand again.

The car came, and Stone's guards shoved him and Holly into the rear seat, while they flagged a cab. "We'll catch up with you," his driver said, "but in a new vehicle."

HALF AN HOUR LATER, Stone and Holly sat in their suite with brandy glasses in hand, trying to come down. There was a hammering on the door, and when Stone answered it, Rick LaRose walked in and locked the door behind him.

"Everybody okay?" he asked.

"Just as soon as we get the brandy down," Stone said. "Pour yourself one."

"I can't find Lance," Rick said, "and he's not answering his phone."

Stone and Holly exchanged a glance. "Lance just needs a little downtime," Holly said. "He'll turn up."

"I even called the ambassador's residence," Rick said.

"Don't worry about it," Stone replied.

"One good thing, though—that van took a beating and came out whole, not even a broken window. It'll see service again."

"I'm so happy for it," Stone said.

"Don't worry, there's a new one downstairs."

"Aren't you running out of them yet?" Holly asked.

"Soon, but not yet. Lance has the authority to requisition replacements."

"Swell," Stone said.

"Did anybody see anything?"

"One of the drivers said the truck driver was dressed in black clothes and wearing heavy boots, like those the police assault teams wear."

"Yeah, Lance told me his theory about Jacques Chance."

"I don't think it's a theory anymore," Stone said.

Stone took a swig of his brandy and sighed.

"What?" Holly asked.

"I was just thinking how nice home would feel at this point."

"Not before we've neutralized Jacques Chance," Rick said.

Holly looked up. "Not before I've worn my new dress to the l'Arrington grand opening."

Stone's phone rang. "Yes?"

"Are you children well?" Lance asked.

"We're still breathing, and nothing is broken."

"Quite a lot like last year's incident, don't you think?"

"Much too much like it."

"The van justified its existence, I'm told."

"It did indeed. How was the rest of your evening, Lance?"

"Stimulating," Lance replied. "And we'll say no more about it."

"As you wish."

"Rick will be there soon with a new one."

"He's already here."

"I've briefed him on the situation with Jacques Chance."

"We've been discussing it."

"Quite soon, now, M'sieur Chance will have his hands full with new problems, and he will be unlikely to be further concerned with you."

"That would be a welcome relief," Stone said.

"And you may get some good news from home. Good night. Read the papers tomorrow morning."

"After I've slept for twelve hours," Stone said, but Lance was already gone. He hung up. "Well, Rick, Lance seems as pleased as punch about how things have gone."

"Lance is a little twisted that way," Rick replied. "I'll say good night. It's unlikely that you two will be assaulted again before morning."

"Only until morning?" Holly asked. "Can't you do better than that?"

"Sweet dreams," Rick said, letting himself out.

Holly came and took Stone's empty glass from him, led him to the bed, undressed him, and tucked him in. "Tell me," she said, adjusting the covers, "do you often have these *déjà vu/ premonition* things?"

"*Déjà vu*, yes. Doesn't everybody? But premonitions, no. My first time."

"Next time, try to have it a bit earlier, like, before we get into the van."

"I'll work on that," Stone said, stroking her hair. "Are you really all right?"

"If I attack you in the morning, then I'm all right. Ask me then."

"I'll be sure and do that," Stone said, drifting off.

The *International New York Times* arrived with breakfast. Stone searched the front page for news of Jacques Chance, but there was nothing.

Holly bit into a croissant. "Maybe the *Times* closes early," she said. "Let's try the French newspapers."

Stone called down for the papers, and they arrived as they were finishing their coffee.

"Here we go," Holly said, holding up a paper.

SCANDALE!

ASSASSIN! CORRUPTION!
ESPIONNAGE RUSSE!

EN HAUT LIEU!

"Now, that's more like it," Holly said.

"May I have a translation, please?"

"Here you go: 'Scandal! Murder! Corruption! Russian Spying!' And all of it 'in High Places!' Or maybe 'Instead of High Places!'"

"That's pretty comprehensive, except that last one doesn't sound quite right."

"My French isn't all that hot," Holly admitted, "but what more could we—correction, Lance—ask for? Look, there's even a mention of Howard Axelrod, a couple of paragraphs down. Apparently, it broke on his website."

Stone scanned the front page and, alarmingly, saw his name mentioned, along with Axelrod, in a box. "What does this say?"

Holly read it a couple of times. "I can't make much sense of it, but they use the word 'excuses.'"

"Axelrod is making excuses for something?" Stone's cell phone rang. "Yes?"

"Good morning," Lance said with enthusiasm. "Seen the papers?"

"Yes, we're looking at them right now. I think we figured out the headlines, but the text is rough going for us, with Holly's French."

"Have you got the *Times*?"

"Yes."

"Page six, bottom half. They didn't play it quite as big."

The headline read "Blogger 'Howard Axelrod' looses salvo in the French Press." Then, in smaller letters, "Apologizes for false rumor about Democratic nominee Katharine Lee.'" Stone read quickly. "Howard Axelrod, as he styles himself, added to his French story an apology to Katharine Lee for a rumor he published claiming that she was pregnant by a man not her husband, New York attorney Stone Barrington. Said Axelrod, 'I relied on a source who turned out to be unreliable. In fact, he has been revealed to be a Republican provocateur who has been instrumental in airing other falsehoods about Mrs. Lee. I apologize, unreservedly, for any distress I have caused both Katharine Lee and her friend Stone Barrington by the publication of this scurrilous fabrication. Neither I nor anyone else has presented the slightest evidence that her child was fathered by anyone but her husband, the president.'"

"How does that sound, Stone?"

"It sounds just wonderful."

"I know you must be relieved."

"I certainly am."

"There is, however, one more step that has to be taken to fully clear your name."

"What's that?"

"We need a news story by a credible, well-placed journalist."

"And how do we do that?"

"Do you remember meeting Carla Fontana last evening? She's the Washington bureau chief for the *New York Times*."

"Yes, of course."

"She has expressed a desire to have dinner with you this evening and interview you about this experience."

"I can see how that could be advantageous."

"However, she doesn't want to be seen interviewing you, so dinner will have to be in your suite at l'Arrington. Must you ask Holly's permission?"

"Hang on." He covered the phone and turned to Holly. "Lance wants me to have dinner with Carla Fontana, of the *Times*, tonight. He thinks she will help to further clear the air." Holly shrugged. "Also, he says I have to see her here—she doesn't want to be seen doing this in public."

Holly's eyebrows shot up. "Aha! Lance wants to get you laid!"

"I don't think that's what he has in mind," Stone said, and went back to the phone. "Okay, Lance, Holly doesn't have a problem with that. What time?"

"She will present herself there at seven P.M. And if sex raises its ugly head, it can't hurt."

"Thanks, Lance, I'll see her then." He hung up.

"You see, he wants to get you into bed with Carla Fontana," Holly said.

"He wants nothing of the sort, and please remember that this was Lance's idea and not mine."

"Okay, I'll clear out for the night. I can bunk at our embassy station. But you wait, I'll bet La Carla is in on it, too."

"Lance says I have to do this to put an end to the story."

"Yeah, sure," Holly said.

S tone was waiting for Carla Fontana to arrive when his cell rang. "Hello?"

"Hey!"

"Hey, Ann, how are you?"

"I am just fine," she said. "Never better, in fact. You are all over the American media, and this time, it's a good thing."

"I read the story in the *International New York Times*."

"It made the front page here, and just about every other front page, too. Kate is delighted, and a flash poll wipes out the earlier losses after Axelrod published the rumor. And you didn't have to take a DNA test on national television!"

"I would have done so, if I'd had to."

"I'll tell Kate you said that. In fact, hold on."

"Stone?"

"Kate? How are you?"

"Ever so much better, thanks. I don't know how you did it, but the apology from Axelrod worked wonders."

"I didn't do it, Lance did."

"Thank him for me."

"Will do. He's also arranged for an interview with Carla Fontana, from the *Times*, so that she can do a story. I'm giving her dinner tonight."

"Excellent. She's a credible reporter, and we have a cordial relationship. However, if you're not careful, *Carla* will be carrying your baby. Take precautions."

"I don't think that will be a problem," Stone said. "How's Will?"

"Much, much better since the paternity issue was so neatly solved. He was getting very tired of the questions."

"I can imagine."

"When are you coming home?"

"In a few days. I have to get the grand opening of l'Arrington out of the way, then I'm free to return."

"Oh, good, you'll be here for election night. I'd like for you to join us at the White House that evening."

"What a wonderful invitation. I'll call the Hay-Adams and book a suite."

"The town will be sold out that night—you're staying with us. How's the Lincoln Bedroom?"

"If you're sure Abe won't mind."

"Believe me, he won't. Is Holly there?"

"She's at the Agency station at the embassy, if you want to reach her."

"No, just tell her I send my love."

"Will do."

"I'll let you go. Your interview must be soon."

"Momentarily."

"Until election night," Kate said, then hung up.

Stone glanced at his watch, then found the room service menu and ordered a sumptuous dinner for two. Then the doorbell rang.

He answered it to find the Washington bureau chief for the *New York Times*, clad in a clinging black dress that revealed an enticing amount of décolletage.

"Good evening, Mr. Barrington," she said.

He ushered her in. "Good evening, Ms. Fontana, and I hope that will be the last time we use that form of address."

"Agreed."

"May I get you something to drink? I have a very nice bottle of Krug on ice."

"That would be perfect." She strolled around the suite's living room and had a peek into the bedroom while he opened the bottle. "This is very impressive," she said. "Do you live this well in all hotels?"

"Just Arringtons," he replied, handing her a fizzing flute.

"That's right, you have a business connection, don't you?"

"I do."

"I'm afraid I won't be here for the grand opening. I have to fly back to New York tomorrow morning."

"I'm sorry to hear that," he said, then breathed a sigh of relief that she and Holly wouldn't be in the same room for the event. "Please have a seat."

She arranged herself becomingly on the sofa and took a sip of her Krug. "Very nice," she said. "I'll enjoy it more after our interview. Why don't we get that out of the way?"

"As you wish."

She removed a small recording device and set it on the sofa table behind them, equidistant from their lips. "Now, background?"

"Born and raised in Greenwich Village, attended P.S. Six, NYU, and NYU Law School."

"How did you get sidetracked into the NYPD?"

"As part of a law school program I rode with a squad car for a few days, and the bug bit. I took the exam, passed, and entered the Academy right after graduation."

"Without taking the bar?"

"After my ride with the NYPD I couldn't imagine ever practicing law. I thought I would be a career police officer."

"And that's where you met our beloved police commissioner?"

"We both made detective in the same class and our captain put us together. We were partners until I left the force ten years later."

"I haven't been able to get the straight story on why you left the NYPD. The official word was a knee injury?"

"That was a convenience for the department. I had made an irritant of myself on a case Dino and I were working, and when I opposed my superiors' views, it became clear I had no future in the department. A police doctor made it official, and I was unceremoniously retired."

"With a seventy-five percent pension, tax-free?"

"That is the reward for being invalided out for a line-of-duty injury. Mine was a gunshot to the knee, from which I had pretty well recovered."

"So you were at loose ends, then?"

"I was doing a renovation job on the town house a great-aunt, my grandmother's sister, had willed to me, so that kept me busy, but I was getting deeper into debt, and my pension wasn't enough. Then I ran into an old classmate from law school . . ."

"That would be William Eggers, managing partner of Woodman & Weld?"

"Correct. Bill suggested that if I would take a cram course for the bar and pass, then he could find some work for me. I did, and I became 'of counsel' to Woodman & Weld."

"What does that mean?"

"Let's go off the record here. In my case, it meant that I was assigned the cases that Woodman & Weld didn't want to deal with and wanted to go away."

"Such as?"

"Such as a client's son who was accused of date rape, a client's wife who while driving intoxicated struck another car and injured someone, or, perhaps hiring a private investigator to help on a difficult divorce. I stress that all these cases are hypothetical."

"I see, and that's how you got something of a reputation as a fixer?"

"All lawyers are fixers—some do it in court, some at the negotiation table, some in other ways."

"And how did you come to have such a reputation with women?"

"I beg your pardon? What kind of reputation are we talking about?"

"A swordsman's reputation, to put it politely. My researcher was able to connect you to more than a dozen women, among them Ann Keaton, a deputy campaign manager for Kate Lee."

"I've spent most of my adult life as a single man," Stone said, "and I have never had any inclination toward celibacy."

She smiled. "An excellent answer. May we talk about how you became a father?"

"Not on the record. My son doesn't need to be reading about that. Perhaps later, off the record and when your recorder isn't operating."

The doorbell rang. "That must be our dinner. I took the liberty of ordering for you."

"Thank you. We can finish our discussion later."

Stone let the waiter in, who set the table and lit the candles.

"Come," Stone said, taking her hand. "Don't let it get cold."

"Nothing will get cold," she said, "I assure you."

39

They began with fresh foie gras, then transitioned to a duck, and another bottle of the Krug was uncorked along the way. Dessert was crème brûlée, and then they were on espresso, which they had on the sofa.

They went back on the record.

"How did you become involved with the Arrington hotels?"

"I had married, and, as I'm sure your researcher has noted, my wife was murdered by a former lover. She was the widow of the actor Vance Calder, and inherited his estate, which included a large plot of land in Bel-Air, Los Angeles. The site seemed ideal for a fine hotel, a corporation was formed and funded, and we opened last year. Then Marcel duBois, whose name I'm sure you know . . ."

"France's Warren Buffett?"

"I've heard him described as such. Marcel contacted me, looking to buy the Bel-Air property, but instead, we went into business together. He already owned the Paris property, which underwent a complete renovation, the result of which you've seen tonight. I came over for the opening."

"My sources tell me that your life has been in danger while you're in Paris."

"I'm afraid I can't discuss that for fear of making things worse."

"All right. How did you and Will and Kate Lee become friends?"

"I was able to be helpful to them on a couple of occasions, and we got along very well. They stayed at the Bel-Air Arrington during the convention last summer."

"And I hear that you were involved in the nominating process?"

"Only in a peripheral way."

"More than one of my sources tell me that you and Ed Eagle were instrumental in Kate's winning the nomination."

"That is a great exaggeration. Please see that I don't get any credit for it in your article."

"As you wish." She switched off her recorder. "And now I must go. I have a nine o'clock flight in the morning, and I have to get up very early to make it." She stood.

Stone stood with her and walked her to the door. "It was a pleasure meeting you," he said.

"I come to New York now and then, for work. Perhaps I'll see you there." She handed him her business card.

"I'll look forward to it," Stone replied, and gave her his own card.

She slipped out the door and was gone.

HE SLEPT until late morning, then had lunch in the suite, then he turned to his e-mail. He found Carla's column among his e-mails, and she had treated him kindly. He scanned the other messages and found one labeled "Axelrod." He opened it and read:

> *This will be my last blog. I am deeply humiliated by the furor caused by my column about Katharine Lee, and as a result, I have decided to discontinue my blog and end my life. One parting note: I've done some digging into the origins of the story: my source, as it turns out, is a lover of Gordon Glenn, a highly placed member of Henry "Honk" Carson's campaign, whose marriage is ending. I think you may draw your own conclusions.*
>
> *Howard Axelrod*

STONE'S cell phone began ringing. "Hello?"

"It's Ann. Have you heard?"

"Heard what?"

She read him the Axelrod blog. "It made the *Times* this morning. Can you believe it?"

"I suppose I have to believe it."

"Gordon Glenn's life will be hell for a few days," she said, "and he deserves it. It's only six A.M. here, but I expect that by nine there'll be a statement from Honk, deploring Glenn's actions and accepting his resignation."

"Have you talked to Kate? Does she know about it?"

"She doesn't get up until seven, and by then it will be all over the morning TV shows, and I'll be releasing a statement saying that she will have no further comment."

"You think this is the end of it, then?"

"How could it not be?"

"You think Axelrod will really kill himself?"

"I think he meant that he was ending Axelrod's life, not his own."

"That makes a lot of sense."

"By the way, Carla Fontana's column about you in the same edition was highly favorable."

"I'm glad to hear it."

"I've gotta run, but I wanted you to know about the column. I wish I knew who Axelrod was."

Stone hung up. He thought he knew.

Shortly after he had received Carla's and Axelrod's columns, Stone's cell phone rang. "Hello?"

"It's Rick."

"Where the hell have you been? You missed a good dinner with Lance."

"In Berlin, talking to people at our station."

"Lance hasn't said a word about the newly wrecked van."

"He's too happy with the story in the French papers to think about anything else."

"Has anyone heard anything from Jacques Chance?"

"He's gone to ground. My journalist friends tell me they haven't been able to get any comment from him, his sister, his father, or the police."

"I can understand why," Stone said. "What do you think of Lance's theory that Jacques is behind the attempts on me?"

"I think it's insane, but probably true."

"Do you think his being exposed will put a stop to the attempts on me?"

"Don't count on it—the people he was acting for are still there and in business. Have you made any arrangements for getting out of town after the shindig at l'Arrington?"

"Not yet, but I will. Will you give Holly a message for me?"

"She's right here—deliver it yourself."

"Good morning," she said.

"Afternoon."

"If you say so."

"I just wanted to tell you, the coast is clear."

"When did it clear?"

"Not too late last night," he lied. "She had an early flight to New York."

"Have you heard about the Howard Axelrod blog?"

"Yes, somebody in New York read it to me."

"And Fontana's column?"

"I hear it's favorable."

"You must have been a good interview."

"I did my best."

"And your best, as we all know, is pretty good."

"Aren't you kind. Will you be back this evening?"

"I'll be there around five. Dinner?"

"Sure. You want to go out?"

"Not really."

"We'll dine in, then."

"See ya." She hung up.

Stone called Mike Freeman at his Paris office.

"Afternoon, Stone. How are you keeping?"

"Fairly busy. You must be, too."

"Yeah, the security arrangements for the l'Arrington opening had to be rethought, in light of all the vehicles you've been losing."

"Yeah, well . . ."

"I can just see Lance explaining it to the Senate Select Committee on Intelligence."

"Let's hope that's not necessary. Surely the Senate doesn't want to hear about every fender bender in the CIA budget."

"I'm sure that's the position he'll take, should it come up. Are you going to need a ride back to New York?"

"I'd like that very much, and Lance would like it, too. He's advised me to decamp."

"I have to be back in New York for a big meeting the day after the opening, so we're planning wheels up afterward, at one A.M. That do you?"

"That do me fine, thanks. Is there room for Holly, should she want to decamp, too?"

"Sure. Leave your packed bags in your suite, and someone will collect them and put them on the airplane. You may want a bag in the cabin so that you can change out of your evening clothes."

"We'll mark one for that."

"If you see Lance, tell him there's room for him, too."

"I'll do that."

"Stone, it's important for my security arrangements that neither you nor Marcel step outside the hotel at any time that evening, not even the courtyard where the cars arrive."

"I will cooperate."

"Something else: Marcel had sent invitations to the Chance family, and they R.S.V.P.'d this morning: the old man won't be there, but Jacques and Mirabelle accepted."

"You astonish me."

"It astonished me, too. Part of my rethinking of the security arrangements is concerned with protecting you from Jacques."

"Do your arrangements involve a metal detector?"

"Of course."

"Then I don't think I'll have anything to worry about."

"Nevertheless."

"Oh, all right."

"See you there." Mike hung up.

Holly breezed in a little after six. "Hey, there!" she said, giving him a wet kiss.

"You're late," Stone said. "I was about to start without you."

"Then I would have had you liquidated, beating the Russians to it."

"Martini?"

"How'd you guess? Hurry up!"

Stone hurried, then handed her the chilled glass and poured himself a Knob Creek.

Holly sank into the living room sofa and kicked off her shoes. Her skirt was up around her thighs, and Stone pretended not to notice.

"I'm bushed," Holly said.

"That is not my recollection," Stone replied.

Holly laughed. "Touché," she said.

"I have a very good memory for these things."

"It remembers you, too," she said.

His hand drifted to her thigh.

"Careful," she said. "You don't want me to spill my martini."

"That's your problem," Stone said, raising his sights.

She gave a little gasp. "Touché again!"

"How is it you are already wet?"

"I was thinking about you in the car."

"What were you thinking?"

"I was remembering something, from about a year ago."

"What was it?"

She told him.

"Ah, yes, I remember it well."

"Isn't that a Lerner and Loewe song?"

"It is. It's also a very pleasant memory."

"That's why I'm wet. Right there, please, that's the spot."

"Do you want me to do that thing again?"

"Yes, but not until after dinner, when we're in bed."

"I'll look forward to it."

"So will I," she said, then she grabbed his arm and made noises of delight.

"That didn't take long," he said.

"Since we have so much time on our hands, do it again."

Stone complied, sipping his bourbon with his other hand.

Holly went limp, nearly spilling her martini. "That was fabulous," she said, "and I still didn't spill a drop."

"You are to be commended for your delicate balance."

"And you are to be commended for your delicate fingers. Do you play the piano?"

"Not for many years."

"You should do it more often," she said. "It would keep you in shape for doing that."

"It was more fun than practicing scales."

"I'm glad it was fun for you, too."

"Entertaining you is always fun."

"'Entertaining.' That's a good way to look at it. It was certainly very that."

"What else can I do for you?" he asked.

"Talk to me, feed me, then we'll start over."

"What would you like to talk about?"

"Is Kate Lee carrying your baby?"

Stone choked on his bourbon. "You've been reading the gutter press," he said.

"The gutter Internet."

"You haven't read the latest."

"What's that? Did I miss something?"

"Howard Axelrod has apologized and committed suicide."

"Shut up!"

Stone got his laptop and showed her the column.

"Well, I'll be damned, and so, I believe, will Axelrod be. Did he really off himself?"

"I think he offed his character."

"Who is he?"

"The man is a mystery to me."

"I'm glad that episode is over. Let's eat."

"What would you like?"

"Shall we have a look at the room service menu?"

"Just think of something—I'll force them to prepare it."

"I'd like a New York strip steak rare, some fried onion rings, some sugar snap peas, and a great California Cabernet. I like it better than the French stuff."

Stone picked up the phone and ordered.

"While we're waiting, some business," she said.

"Shoot."

"My New York station has suddenly discovered that I can speak, even when I'm out of town, so they've been on the phone all day."

"Anything you can tell me about?"

"My friend Scott, over at the NSA, has been surfing the metadata for Russian mob stuff, and your name came up."

"In what regard?"

"In what regard do you think?"

"Something to do with my demise, no doubt."

"Bingo!"

"Anything specific?"

"The word 'gala' was mentioned. Or whatever the Russian for 'gala' is."

"I'm scheduled for only one gala," Stone said.

"I know, and since I plan to accompany you, wearing my

new dress, I'm going to take particular care to see that you end the evening in the same condition as you start it."

"That's very kind of you. Mike Freeman has similar intentions."

"Not quite the same as mine," she said.

"By the way, the Strategic Services Gulfstream 650 departs Le Bourget at one A.M., after the gala. Mike says both you and Lance are welcome to bum a ride."

"There's a bed on that airplane, isn't there?"

"Now that you mention it, yes."

"I'll be there," she said.

42

Stone's cell phone rang a little after eight. Holly was still sleeping soundly. "Hello?"

"Mr. Barrington?" A woman's voice. "I'm calling for Marcel duBois."

"Yes?"

"He would be very pleased if you would join him for breakfast at his home. He has something important to discuss with you."

Stone checked the bedside clock. "Of course. What time?"

"As soon as you can be here."

"Give me half an hour," he said. He tiptoed out of the room, shaved, showered, and dressed, then went downstairs. The courtyard was empty of his usual transport. He thought of calling Rick LaRose, then thought better of it and got into a cab. Ten minutes later he was deposited in the courtyard of the duBois building. Two security types loitered near the door, but neither was dressed in the usual body armor. One of them gave him a little salute as he approached the door, then held it open for him. Stone had a good memory for faces, but he didn't recognize the guard.

He rode the elevator upstairs and got off at the top level, where Marcel's apartment was. "Marcel?" he called.

"In here," duBois responded.

Stone walked through the living room and into Marcel's study. The Frenchman sat in an armchair next to a man Stone didn't recognize. He heard a small noise behind him and turned to find two hefty men sporting bulges under their arms.

"Stone Barrington," Marcel said, "this is Yevgeny Majorov." He nodded at his other guest.

"How do you do?" Stone asked, thinking fast. He was out of options at the moment.

"I do very well, Mr. Barrington," Majorov said. "Please have a seat. I'm told breakfast will be ready in a moment." His accent was more British than Russian.

As he spoke, a uniformed butler wheeled a large table into the room and uncovered several dishes.

"It's a buffet," Majorov said.

"I recognized it," Stone replied.

The three men served their plates and sat down at a table already set for them.

"How did they get in?" Stone asked Marcel.

"I don't know," the Frenchman replied.

"Fear not, Mr. Barrington," Majorov said, "I'm unarmed and not here to harm you."

"What about your two minions?" Stone asked, jerking a thumb toward the men.

"They harm only those who attempt to harm me."

"That's benevolent of them. How many people did you harm getting into the building?"

"It was done quickly and quietly," Majorov said, "and without serious injury to any person."

Stone didn't believe that for a moment.

They ate quietly for a bit, then Majorov spoke up. "I'm here on business," he said.

"What sort of business?"

"I know that, in the past, you have rejected offers from my organization."

"Quite true. Why do you think anything has changed?"

"Because the leadership of my organization has changed."

"In what respect?"

"I am now its chief executive, instead of my late brother."

"I fail to see the difference."

"My brother tended toward bluntness in business and relied on violence instead of negotiation to achieve his ends."

"I'm acquainted with his techniques."

"My brother also tended toward the lowball offer when seeking new assets."

"Yes."

"When I took charge of the organization I began a top-to-bottom reorganization, eliminating a number of older members who relied on my brother's techniques to achieve success. The Neanderthals are gone."

"Leaving what?"

"Civilized men, like myself, who wish to conduct our affairs in a more straightforward manner."

"Like the two—no, three recent attempts on my life?"

"I wish to apologize for that. We had previously relied on a French national who tended to overstep."

"That would be Jacques Chance?"

"Regrettably, yes. I should mention that his actions were exacerbated by your attentions to his sister. As a result, we have severed all ties to him. He was a holdover from my brother's regime, and even so, we regard his actions as business, not personal."

Stone ignored the Mafia-esque reference. "Frankly, after Jacques's sudden disappearance from public life, I was surprised to hear that he was still alive."

"You may put that down to regime change," Majorov said. "I hope his absence from the scene will clear the air between us and allow us to do business on a more normal basis."

"You can hope."

Marcel suppressed a laugh. "Perhaps, Stone, we can hear out Mr. Majorov, then discuss it between us."

"As you wish, Marcel."

"First of all," Majorov said, "I am willing to put aside your involvement in the death of my brother."

"I had no such involvement," Stone said, "in spite of his repeated attempts on my life and that of my son and his friends."

"I have good reason to attach the involvement of an associate of yours to my brother's death," Majorov said, sounding angry for the first time.

"And whom would that be?"

"A fugitive from American justice named Theodore Fay, I believe."

"You may believe what you wish," Stone said, "but I have good reason to believe that no such person exists."

"Perhaps you know him under another name?"

"And what name would that be?"

Majorov reddened. "I have been unable to discover that, but I am sure that he exists and that he killed not only my brother, but at least four of his associates."

"Are you referring to the men who were attempting to kill my son and his friends in Arizona?"

"Again, you are referring to a regime in my organization that no longer exists. May we not begin anew with a clean slate?"

"We may not," Stone said.

"Stone," Marcel interjected, "let's hear what Mr. Majorov has to say."

"If you insist, Marcel."

"Mr. Barrington," Majorov said, "my organization has acquired a majority position in a chain of fine hotels in Russia and Eastern Europe called the Ikon Group."

"I know these hotels," Marcel said. "They are fairly good hostelries, but they could use much improvement."

"We are prepared to make that investment," Majorov said, "and we are prepared to make an attractive offer for the Arrington Group, whose expertise would be of benefit to us in refining our hotels. Our offer would be a sum greater than the current value of your hotels."

"By whose standards?" Marcel asked.

"By objective assessments by real estate experts in Los Angeles and Paris."

"All right, Marcel," Stone said, "I have heard out Mr. Majorov, and now I wish to say that I have no interest in any offer from his organization and no interest in hearing further from Mr. Majorov on the subject of our hotels—or on any other subject, for that matter." He turned to Majorov. "Do I make myself perfectly clear?"

Majorov was redder, now, and his hands trembled slightly as he spoke. "Perfectly clear," he said. "But I wish you to remember that I made this offer in good faith, and that you insulted me."

"I rejected your offer," Stone said. "Any insult is your inference."

Majorov stood, knocking over a glass at his table setting. His two companions swiftly moved to either side of him.

Stone was eyeing a sharp-looking knife on the table.

"I should tell you, Mr. Barrington," Majorov said, "that the conflict in my organization has not entirely ended, and that there are still those who would regard your absence from the scene as beneficial."

"I should tell you, Mr. Majorov," Stone replied, "that I will hold you entirely responsible for any further attempt on the persons of M'sieur duBois or myself or any of our associates or properties. And you may regard that as personal, not business."

Majorov threw his napkin onto the table and stalked from the room, accompanied by his two bodyguards.

"Whew!" Marcel said. "That man appeared in my bedroom this morning and frightened me half to death. I thought you dealt with him brilliantly."

"I don't think either of us is through dealing with him," Stone said.

43

Stone had a cup of coffee with Marcel and tried to calm him down. When he went downstairs there were no guards present outside the building. He went back inside and looked around the ground floor, then he heard a banging noise and traced it to a closed door. He opened it and found a supply closet containing half a dozen people, bound and gagged, sitting on the floor.

Stone freed one of them and told him to free the others. "Then I suggest you resume your posts and do your work with more care." He left the building and found a cab in the street. Strangely, he found comfort in being in an ordinary taxi rather than an armored van. "Saint-Germain-des-Prés," he said to the driver in his best French, which he knew made him sound like an American schoolboy working on his pronunciation.

He wanted a day off from all this. He got out of the cab in front of the old church and began to walk, window-shopping in galleries as he went. He entered a small shop and bought a small sculpture he had seen in the window and asked that it be shipped to his home in New York. He walked for another two hours, then had a good lunch in a small restaurant. His cell phone rang several times, but he ignored it.

He passed a cinema and, on a whim, bought a ticket and saw a film in French with English subtitles, no doubt a nod to the tourists. He lost himself in the film, and when he came outside the November day was beginning to lose its light.

He stopped in another gallery and bought a picture, then he resolved to walk back to the Arrington. He was crossing a bridge over the Seine, and he stopped to have a good look at the Eiffel Tower, watching its light show. Then he looked around and found that he was alone on the bridge. Each end was blocked by black SUVs, and from both sides, men in dark clothes were approaching him. He caught a glimpse of an assault rifle and realized he had no place to go.

Then the men walking toward him began to run, and Stone took the only escape available to him. He placed his hands on the bridge's railing and vaulted over it. The dark water rushed up at him, and he managed to enter it feet first, having no idea how far he had fallen. He grabbed a breath as the icy Seine closed over him, and he resolved to stay under as long as he could. He experienced a detailed flashback of the experience of the night before with Holly in bed, which seemed to last several minutes. He must be dying, he thought, even though it was not his life flashing before him, but visions of Holly's body.

He broke the surface, gasping for breath. He could not have been underwater for more than half a minute, he guessed, but the bridge seemed far away. Men were running in both directions, and some were looking down into the water. He had not realized how swift was the Seine's current, nor how cold it was. His strength was being sapped by the chill and his trench coat seemed to be pulling him down. Still, he didn't shrug it off; it might contain a little body heat. A barge was bearing down on him, and he swam a few strokes to get out of its way. He had not got far enough, though, and he found himself being bumped along the length of its hull. He saw a tire coming toward him, suspended from the barge's deck by a short rope, and he managed to get an arm through it.

Now he was being towed downstream, and his feet rose to the surface, trailing behind him. He reached up and got hold of a large cleat, from which the tire was suspended, and hoisted himself high enough to get a foot inside the tire. With his last strength he used the tire as his ladder and pulled himself onto the narrow deck. Then he knew nothing.

NEXT, he heard a woman's voice. "Pierre!" she was shouting, over and over. "Pierre, *venez!*" Stone stared up into an upside-down face, then he passed out again.

When he woke for the second time, he was warm. He was under a heavy blanket—no, several blankets—in a small cabin. He sat up and looked around. There was a little chest of drawers built into one wall, and there were framed pictures resting on it, family photographs. He stood up and found that he was naked, and he wrapped one of the blankets around himself. He peeked out the door and saw a hallway leading aft to what seemed to be a saloon. "Hello!" he called out. "*Bon soir!*" No reply. His words had been lost in the sound of the barge's rumbling engine. He staggered down the hallway and emerged into the nautical version of a family living room. A woman stood with her back to him, bent over an ironing board. On a table behind her was a little pile of things that had once been in his pockets—a credit card case, euros held by a large gold paper clip, a comb, and his iPhone.

"Pardon!" he shouted, and she turned around. She was perhaps fifty, with a weathered but handsome face, dressed in a flannel shirt and jeans. "*Mon Dieu!*" she said.

"No," Stone said, "just an American. *Parlez-vous Anglais?*"

"*Oui,*" she said. "Ah, yes, pretty good. You would like some soup?"

"*Merci*, yes, please."

She went to the galley and returned with a large mug containing a dark, steaming liquid: onion soup, as it turned out.

He sipped some. "*Wunderbar,*" he sighed, and she laughed.

"You are *Deutsch*? Ah, German?"

"No, just a poor linguist."

She laughed again.

"Who is Pierre? I heard you calling to him."

"My husband. He is in the wheelhouse."

"Where are we?"

"Half the time to the Channel *Anglais*. Where have you come from?"

He thought about that. He couldn't think of the name of the bridge. "A bridge," he said.

"Are you, ah, suicide?"

Stone laughed. "No, but some people were trying to help me in that direction."

"Why?"

"It's a long story," he said.

She shrugged. "Not my business," she said. "You were very lucky to get on our barge. You did not seem wounded, so we did not call for the ambulance."

"I certainly was very lucky." The soup was cooling, and he drank some more. "You make very good soup."

"Thank you. When you have drink it all, you may get into your clothes. I am having dried them."

He looked behind her and saw his shirt and underwear, ironed and neatly stacked. "Thank you so much," he said. His suit hung on a hanger, and his trench coat on a peg.

"Your coat takes a little longer, but you can get dressed." She turned her back and resumed ironing something.

Stone got into his underwear, socks, trousers, and shirt. "Did I have shoes?" he asked.

She went to the galley oven and produced them, stuffed with newspaper. "They are toast," she said.

"They'll do. He put them on, and his feet warmed. He picked up his iPhone and turned it on, but it didn't react.

"Your Apple does not like our river," she said.

He put his belongings into his pockets, and she took down his trench coat and began ironing it.

"Our Seine is dirty," she said, "but we have, how you say, all mod cons."

"A washer and dryer," he said.

"Yes. Have you hunger?"

He picked up his Rolex from the table and consulted it. It was just past midnight. "Yes, I'm hungry, thank you." He slipped the watch on and secured it. He found his signet ring on the table, too, and put it on his left pinkie. "There," he said, "I'm back together."

"Your cravat did not fare well," she said.

"I have other cravats. I'm very grateful for your help." He offered his hand. "My name is Stone Barrington."

"I am Madeleine Le Croix," she said.

A man's voice boomed out. "*Qui est-ce?*"

"Mr. Barrington," his wife said. "*Un Americain.*"

The two men shook hands.

"We see all things in the Seine," Pierre said. "This is the first time a guest."

Madeleine went to the galley and came back with a bowl of dark stew. "Pot au feu," she said, handing it to him.

They sat down at the table and Stone ate. "You are a wonderful cook," he said. "Who else is on board?"

"Our son, Jean—he sail the boat," Pierre said. "You are very tired—go and sleep more. We stop in Rouen to leave some cargo, then to Le Havre. You can go back to Paris from Rouen, if you wish it." He smiled. "Or perhaps that is not so good an idea?"

"Thank you, I'll think that over." Stone went back to the cabin and stretched out on the berth. When he woke again, sun was streaming through a porthole, and he smelled bacon cooking.

They docked in an area with a church and shops.
Stone met the son, Jean, then the parents walked
him down the gangplank to the pontoon.

"There is a taxi stand near the church," Pierre said, pointing. "It is ten minutes to the station. Not all the trains go to Paris."

"I'll keep that in mind." Stone thanked them, shook their hands, and walked toward the taxi stand. On the way he passed a wine shop; he went in, chose a case of very good burgundy, paid for it, and asked the proprietor to deliver it to the barge, then he continued his walk. He passed a post office, went in and asked for a telephone. He was sent to a booth where he called the American Embassy and asked for Rick LaRose, since Rick's direct number was in his dead iPhone.

"There is no such person in the embassy," the operator replied.

"He's the CIA station chief," Stone said. "Tell him Stone Barrington is on the line."

After a long moment: "Stone, is that you?"

"It is," Stone said.

"Where the hell are you? We lost track of you yesterday, when you left the hotel. Holly said you didn't come home last night."

"I'm in Rouen," Stone said. "I'll explain when I see you. Will you have me met at the station in Paris?"

"From Rouen that will be the Gare du Nord."

"I suppose so. I don't want to go back to the hotel immediately, and I don't want another of your Mercedes tanks—they attract attention."

"We'll have you met and keep you safe."

"By the way, that very handy iPhone that Lance gave me has not survived the experience. I could use a new one."

"What experience?"

"Later."

"What train?"

"Check the schedule. I'll get the next available. I'm ten minutes from the station."

"All right."

Stone hung up, walked to the taxi stand, and rode to the station. The next train was in twenty minutes, so he bought an *International New York Times* and sat on a bench to read it. There was a report on page three of an altercation on a Paris bridge involving armed men, and a man was said to have leapt into the Seine and had not been seen again.

THE TRAIN wasn't the fast one, but it was fast enough. Stone did the crossword and kept an eye out for suspicious characters, though it seemed very unlikely that anyone might know where he was. As he got off the train at the Gare du Nord, he saw Rick waiting for him. They shook hands.

Rick waited until they were in the back of an Audi sedan before questioning him. "All right," he said, "let's have it."

Stone told him about breakfast with Yevgeny Majorov.

"I would have not thought that possible," Rick said, "what with the security arrangements at the duBois building."

"Neither would I. I'll have to explain it all to Mike Freeman."

"Oh, they were not Mike's people," Rick said. "Marcel reverted to his own means, to his regret, I'm sure."

"When I left I decided to have a day on the town."

"In a cab?"

"It felt more normal. I did some shopping and saw a movie, then, when I was walking back across a bridge, they blocked traffic and came at me from both ends. I took refuge in the Seine."

"Good God! Do you know how fast and how cold that river is?"

"I do now. I caught a ride on a barge, and the crew were kind to me. They docked at Rouen, and I called you. Where are we going?"

"Not to the embassy or the hotel," Rick said. "We have a safe house for you."

"Does Holly know I'm alive?"

"I let her know. I had the impression she thought you had gotten a better offer."

Stone laughed. "Hardly!"

AFTER a few minutes' drive they stopped at a pair of tall, oaken doors, where two men stood guard, and Rick identified himself. The doors were opened and closed behind them; they were in a mews, and they pulled into a garage. Once the door was closed behind them, Rick used a key to let them into the adjoining house. He handed the key to Stone, along with a new iPhone. "The phone already has your contacts and apps in it."

Stone gave him the dead phone. "Maybe it can be resurrected."

"Don't leave the mews except in the company of the two

men on guard," he said. "We'll talk later." He left by way of the garage.

Stone walked into the house and found himself in a small kitchen. He continued into a living room where there was a fire going. Holly sat in a chair beside it, sipping something from a cup.

"All right," she said, "let's have it. I'm looking forward to your explanation."

45

S tone sat in water up to his chin, a glass of Knob Creek resting on the rim of the tub, the heat soaking into his bones, Holly's foot in his crotch, doing things with her toes.

She took a sip of her martini. "A likely story," she said. "Do you really expect me to believe that?"

"Go take a look at my suit and trench coat," Stone replied. "And remember, what you see is *after* they were cleaned and pressed."

"You have other suits," she said. "I packed your things and brought your luggage here. Everything is in the master dressing room. Are you sure you jumped and were not pushed?"

"In another few seconds I would have been *dumped*. I just took the shortcut and stayed alive."

"Why did you pass out?"

"I've wondered about that. I think it was just exhaustion, both times."

"And this woman who took care of you—she was beautiful, wasn't she?"

"In her way, yes, but not the way you mean."

"I'm trying not to be jealous."

"You, jealous? I don't believe it."

"Somewhere along the way, you seem to have forgotten that I'm a woman."

"I have *never* lost sight of that fact—I just thought you were a more liberated woman."

"I am entirely liberated, right up to the point where another woman enters the picture."

"Like the ambassador?"

"That's different—that was just funny."

"I like this house," Stone said, waving his bourbon at the beautifully tiled, old-fashioned bathroom.

"A station chief once owned it. The Agency bought it from him, furnished, when he departed for Afghanistan. What with the mews and the big doors, it makes a good safe house."

"How many bedrooms?"

"Four—three of them are on the top two floors. There's a little staff flat on the other side of the garage."

"And the master?"

"Takes up the whole second floor. There's a nice study, too, that you haven't seen, yet."

"I want to live here."

"Make Lance an offer."

Stone sighed. "I'm dreaming. I'm an American, and I live very well in New York. And anyway, you're in New York."

"No, I'm in Agency purdah. I can't think of anything else but work when I'm in New York. That's why it's so much fun being in Paris: I'm free!" She sighed. "Except for the phone."

"Turn it off," Stone said.

"I daren't. If I don't answer, people come looking for me."

"You're a slave to the CIA."

"I know it, and they know it."

"Why do you go on like this?"

"Because what I do matters—bad people die and good people live. I make the world a better place."

"Really?"

She gave a rueful shrug. "Well, sometimes, and sometimes is good enough for me."

"I can't argue with that," Stone said. "Nothing I can offer you is as good."

"If we were together all the time, it wouldn't be as good as it is right now: it's the desert that makes the oasis so attractive."

"I think I've soaked enough, outside and in," he said. "Now I want to dry you with a big, soft towel and take you to bed. I want to sleep, because I can't stay awake any longer. When I awaken, I'll make it all up to you."

"I'll hold you to that," Holly said, standing up in the tub, the water streaming from her body.

Stone stood up, too, and went to work with the towel.

STONE WOKE early the next morning—at least, it seemed early. There was light coming through the space between the curtains. He got up and pulled the cord, and cloudy daylight filled every corner of the room. There was the canopied bed and the sofa before the fireplace, now cold. There were a couple of comfortable chairs, with reading lamps beside them, bookcases on either side of the fireplace, bare of books.

There was a note on the bedside table. *I had to run and I was loath to wake you—you were sleeping like a small boy. There's breakfast in the kitchen fridge. All you have to do is switch on the coffeepot and warm the croissants. Lunch is there, too. For God's sake, don't leave the house, not until we've cleared the Paris air. I'll be back in time for dinner.*

Stone got into a robe and slippers, went down to the kitchen, and made breakfast, then he went into the living room. He found it the least attractive room in the house; the furnishings had been overused and underrepaired. He walked into the adjacent study; he liked that a lot better.

He had plans to make; he had to turn anger into revenge; he had to end this. He had no idea how, but it would come to him. In the meantime, he had some shopping to do.

S tone walked out of the cottage and down the mews
to the big doors. There was a small door inside one
of them, and he let himself out. His two guards
were surprised.

"Mr. Barrington," one of them said, "you're not supposed
to go out."

"Not true," Stone replied. "I'm not supposed to go out without you two. Follow me, but don't crowd me." He started down
the Boulevard Saint-Germain, window-shopping along the
way. He had previously noted the home-furnishing shops in
the street, and he stopped before an unusual one. Instead of
the latest in modern design, this one was filled with older,
more interesting things. He walked in.

A tall, gray-haired woman got up from a rocking chair and put her book down. She regarded him, up and down, for a moment, then, in American English, she said, "What can I do for you?"

"Ah, you speak my mother tongue," Stone said. He guessed she was in her seventies.

"That's because I'm from your mother country," she replied. "New York. How about you?"

"You're from my mother city, too," he said. "How long in Paris?"

"Fifty years, next month," she said. "I'm Chey Stefan."

"I'm Stone Barrington." They shook hands. "All those years in this shop?"

"I was an actress. I grew older while the roles grew younger, so I morphed into the stylist business."

"Stylist business?"

"There are two kinds of stylists," she said, "one for clothes and the other for rooms. I style rooms."

"How does that work?"

"Suppose a director shoots some scenes in a house. It's a nice house, but not nice enough. I make it nicer, then I rent them the furnishings by the day."

"Do you also sell the furnishings?"

"That's what this shop is for," she said. "What do you need?"

"I need to turn a nice room into a great one," Stone said, "and I need to have it done by five o'clock today. Can you manage that?"

"I'm probably the only person in the arrondissement who can," she said. "See anything you like?"

Stone walked around a well-used but very handsome leather sofa and sat down. "I like this," he said. "And that chair." He pointed, then walked over and sat in it. It was covered in what looked like a Shetland tweed.

"It's one of a pair."

"I'll have them both," he said. "And those two end tables and those lamps over there. I need a brass reading lamp, too."

She walked to the back of the room and stood next to one. "Like this?"

"Exactly like that."

"You're easy. What else do you need?"

"A good rug, about twelve by eighteen."

"Feet or meters?"

"Feet."

"Follow me." She led him into a back room and to a large rack that held rugs, hung up like towels in a bathroom.

Stone walked over to a rug. "Size?"

She consulted a tag. "Fourteen by twenty-two."

"That will do." He turned and saw that the wall behind him was covered by a huge bookcase, filled with leather-bound and good cloth volumes. "And books," he said.

"I sell them by the yard, in French or English. There are more a couple of rooms back."

"I'll take twenty yards of English, a mix of leather and cloth, whatever is beautiful."

She made notes on a pad.

Another wall was covered in pictures: landscapes, still lifes, nudes, and portraits. Stone began pointing while she took more notes.

"I like the table there, too."

More notes.

"And I need a grand piano. I don't suppose you can do that."

"Right this way," she said, and led him to yet another room. Three grand pianos stood, covered by sheets. She whisked them away. "Do you play?"

"Some, but not for a long time."

There was a monstrously French gilt instrument, another black-lacquered, and one of walnut. "The Bechstein has the nicest tone," she said, indicating the walnut instrument.

Stone sat down and played a few chords, then struck individual keys high and low. "Very nice. Needs a tuning."

"That can be done immediately."

They walked back into the first room, and Stone picked a few objets d'art and a pair of mahogany wastebaskets.

"I think that will do," Stone said. "I'll need your eye to style the room, too, and I'll need you to take away what's there. You can sell it or junk it."

"Where is all this going?"

"Couple of hundred yards down the street, there are a pair of oak doors guarding a mews. In the mews house, please."

He looked at his watch. He gave her the street number. "How long?"

"By four o'clock," she said.

"How much for everything?" he asked.

She sat down at a desk and began flicking through her notes, tapping numbers into a computer. "I'll give you a bulk discount," she said, and named a number.

"Done," he said.

"Shall I call the piano tuner?"

"Please." He gave her his business card and wrote down his cell number. "I'll be waiting," he said.

"Not for long," she replied, accepting his AmEx card.

47

Stone stood in the mews and shook Chey Stefan's hand. "I want to thank you for doing such a beautiful job, and for doing it so quickly."

"It was my pleasure," Chey said, "and I thank you for your business." She got into the moving van containing the former living room furnishings and drove away. The guards closed the big doors behind her.

Stone walked into his new living room and looked around. The furniture, the pictures, the books, and the fresh flowers Chey had brought as a gift made the place feel as if he had always lived there. He sat down at the newly tuned Bechstein grand and began to play an old Irving Berlin song, "All Alone," that he particularly loved.

"Freeze," someone behind him said.

He froze. Someone had got past the guards.

"Who are you," she asked, "and what have you done with Stone Barrington?"

Stone turned slowly to find Holly in a firing stance, a handgun held in front of her with both hands. "Welcome home," he said.

Holly lowered the gun slowly. "What the hell is going on here? This place is completely different from the one I left this morning."

"Nicer, isn't it?"

She looked around. "Well, yes, it's a lot nicer."

"I just rearranged the furniture."

"You did a lot more than that. There wasn't a grand piano in this room when I left."

"By rearranged, I meant that I moved the old furniture out and the new furniture in."

Holly came and sat next to him on the piano bench. "Another thing," she said, "how did you learn to play the piano in a single day?"

"I told you, I've always played," he said, "just not for a long time. I got out of the habit."

"Well, it's a very nice habit."

"It's your fault that I bought the piano. You said I should play to keep my fingers in shape for other work."

She laughed. "I did say that, didn't I?"

Stone flexed his fingers. "Ready for duty."

"I want a drink first," she said. "I'll fix one for you, too."

She went to the wet bar, made a martini, and brought it back with a bourbon for Stone. "Play," she said.

Stone played "The Way You Look Tonight."

"That's my favorite song," she said. "How'd you know?"

"I just knew."

They sipped their drinks and Stone played some more. The tunes kept flooding back.

"That was lovely," she said, when he paused. "But stop for a minute while I ruin the mood."

"What's wrong?"

"Rick has had word that Majorov's people think you may still be alive and are scouring the city for you. He wants me to move you to the country right now. I have a car waiting."

"Just a minute," Stone said. He produced his new iPhone and looked for Lance Cabot's number, then dialed it."

"What strange person is calling on one of my phones?" Lance asked.

"It's Stone. My old phone died."

"It must have drowned, from what I hear."

"Your information is good."

"Why have you honored me with this call, Stone? I have people in my office."

"I'll be brief: You know the little mews house I'm sequestered in?"

"I do, and it's not so little."

"I want to buy it from you."

"*What?*"

"Come on, Lance, how much do you want for it?"

"It's owned by the same Agency foundation that sold you your cousin Dick Stone's house."

"And you are the chairman of its board, authorized to act for it, as I recall. You did that when I bought the Maine house."

"That's true, I suppose."

"Come on, Lance, I'll let you make a small profit on the place, so you'll look good for the board. How much did you pay?"

"It was some time ago: a million four, I think. Euros."

"I'll give you a million five, and I'll bet it was dollars."

"No, it was euros, I'm sure. A million six, and it's yours. Euros."

"Oh, all right, done, but fully furnished."

"Anything that's there. There's a car, too, in the garage."

"So that's what's under the sheet."

"It's an old Mercedes, I believe. The Paris station keeps it running."

"I'll have my office send you a check made out to the foundation and a sales contract, probably tomorrow or the next day."

"Done, then. It's yours from this moment on."

"Nice doing business with you, Lance." Stone hung up.

Holly was staring at him agape. "Did you really just do that?"

"You know, when I inherited Arrington's fortune, I was very uncomfortable with the idea of spending any of it."

"But you got over it," Holly pointed out.

"The great thing about being filthy rich is that you can make snap judgments and write a check. Speaking of that, excuse me." He called home.

"The Barrington Practice," Joan said.

"You're supposed to say, 'Woodman & Weld,'" Stone pointed out.

"I forgot. You okay?"

"Never better. Listen, I just bought a little mews house in Paris."

"Ooh! Can I come for a visit?"

"Later. Call Herbie Fisher and have him find an attorney at W&W's Paris office and have him write a sales contract and do whatever they do in France, like a title search. The seller is the same foundation that sold me the Maine house." He gave her the street address of the mews house. "When he's drawn it, have him FedEx it to Lance Cabot at the CIA, and you send him a cashier's check for a million, six hundred thousand euros, in dollars. I'd like Lance to have it all the day after tomorrow. They can e-mail the contract to you, and you can send it all together."

"Consider it done," Joan said.

"I miss you terribly," he replied, and hung up before she could reply. "There," he said to Holly.

"That was breathtaking," she said, draining her martini glass. "Now, how are your fingers feeling?" she asked.

"Rejuvenated."

"Then come with me," she said, taking his hand.

S tone lay with his head cradled in Holly's breasts. "That was wonderful," he said.

"I'm impressed with the current condition of your fingers," she said. "Maybe you don't need to play the piano after all. How on earth could you just stop doing that?"

"I played in a jazz group in college, but I had to quit when I started law school—there just wasn't time. Then years passed without a piano, and when I finally got one for the New York house, I was too busy to play."

"Okay, I'll buy that. Now it's time for us to get out of here."

"I'm not going anywhere," Stone said. "This house is now my home in Paris, and I'm not moving out to avoid Yevgeny

Majorov. In fact, I don't want to avoid Yevgeny Majorov, I want to kill him."

"I'm entirely in sympathy with that desire, nevertheless, we have to think about your safety, as well as his demise. Leave that to Rick and his boys."

"Look, we have no reason to believe that Yevgeny knows where I am."

"You might have been spotted when you went furniture shopping today."

"Or I might not have been spotted, or they would be here by now. Anyway, if I leave here again, that increases the chances of his people spotting me."

"Well, there is a kind of logic in that," she admitted.

Stone's cell phone rang, and he reached for it on the bedside table. "Hello?"

"It's Rick. Why are you still there?"

"I live here, and I'm not going anywhere."

"Nobody lives in a safe house—you stay as long as you're safe, then you move to another safe house."

"This is no longer a safe house."

"That's my point."

"No, I mean it's *my* house—I bought it from Lance."

A short silence. "Lance doesn't own it."

"The foundation owns it, and Lance is the head of the foundation's board of trustees and has the authority to sell it. In fact, it will be the second house the foundation has sold me. A contract is being drawn as we speak."

"I'm sorry," Rick said, "I'm getting dizzy."

"Focus on a fixed object, like my presence in this house."

"It's dangerous for you there."

"Why?"

"Because we've spotted some of Majorov's people cruising the seventh arrondissement, looking for you."

"They haven't found me yet, but if I leave here, that gives them another shot."

Rick sighed. "All right, then I'll send some firepower over there."

"I just started refurnishing the place, and I don't want it shot up."

"Then I'll place them on nearby roofs."

"You've already got two of your boys on me—three, with Holly."

"Thanks a lot," Holly said. "I thought you knew the difference between boys and girls."

Stone bit her on a nipple.

"Ow!"

"You loved that."

"I loved what?" Rick asked.

"Never mind. May I suggest that you stop concentrating on defense and switch to offense. It's time to stop screwing with this guy and put him permanently out of business."

"There are more where he came from."

"If they keep losing management, they'll eventually get discouraged and look for somebody else's hotels to steal."

"I don't know about that, they've been remarkably persistent."

"Tell me about it—that's why I want it ended, and I don't care if the gutters of Paris run red with their blood."

"I also have to keep your blood out of the gutters. Going to war with these people won't fix it."

"Cutting the head off the snake might."

Rick made a strangled noise. "I'll talk to Lance."

"You do that. Bye." Stone hung up.

"I guess we're hunkering down here," Holly said.

He kissed a nipple. "And we hunker so well, don't we?"

His phone rang again. "Hello?"

"It's Herb Fisher."

"Hey, Herb, how are you?"

"I'm just fine, thanks. What's this about your moving to Paris?"

"Nobody said anything about moving here—I just found a place I liked, so I bought it."

"I spoke to an Yves Carrier in our Paris office, and he's on it. He's doubtful about as quick a transaction as you want."

"I just want to get Lance Cabot's signature on a suitable document and to pay him before he has second thoughts."

"We can do that, but there may be other formalities that will have to be dealt with before you'll own it in the eyes of the French. They have a large bureaucracy there, and they have to give them work to do."

"Tell M'sieur Carrier to take as long as it takes for that stuff—just the transaction done in the eyes of the CIA. Joan's already getting a cashier's check that will be on his desk when he gets the e-mailed document. All he has to do is print it and sign it, then deposit the check, and we're done, as far as I'm concerned."

"Are you still at l'Arrington?"

"No, I'm in the house, but keep that to yourself. I had to leave l'Arrington because people were looking for me there, so tell M'sieur Carrier to keep his lip buttoned."

"Okay. When are you coming back?"

"Later this week, after the grand opening of the hotel."

"See you then."

They both hung up.

"What are we doing about dinner?" Stone asked.

"I stopped by Fauchon on the way here and got us some prepared dishes. All we have to do is nuke them."

Stone got a leg over. "First, I have to nuke you."

Ann Keaton called the unruly meeting to order. "Hey! Shut up!" Reluctantly, they did. "And cut those phones off and put them away!" Resentfully, they did.

"We've got a new poll, and Tom Alpert is here to explain it." There was a collective groan.

Tom Alpert was a skinny man in a black suit; he looked like an undertaker. "I've been told I look like an undertaker," he said. "That may be appropriate for this meeting."

Now everybody was really, really quiet and attentive.

"I want to stress that this wasn't done on the fly. We have a sample of twelve thousand independent, likely voters in seventeen swing states, and here's how it breaks down: if the election were held today, fifty-four percent of them would vote for Honk, excuse me, Henry Carson. Forty-four percent would vote for Kate Lee, with two percent undecided. That is a *very* small number of undecideds at this stage. If Kate won all of them, we could lose the election by as much as eight points."

There were expressions around the table ranging from disbelief to near tears.

"Wait a minute," somebody said. "Between Democrats and Republicans we're holding at fifty-five percent Dems to forty-six percent Reps, aren't we?"

"Not anymore," Alpert said. "The numbers won't be in until the day after tomorrow, but we know the margin is narrowing. What I'm saying is, we're on the knife's edge of losing, and the personal conduct of the candidates could throw it either way. If either of them does or says something stupid in the next few days, it could make the difference."

Ann spoke up. "Kate is not known for making stupid statements or behaving stupidly," she said. "Honk, on the other hand . . ."

"Don't count on that happening this week," Alpert said. "Honk won't say a word that isn't typed in great big letters into a teleprompter—you may count on that." He cleared his throat. "I would advise Kate to do the same."

"Kate hates prompters," Ann said, "and she's *very* good on her feet."

"Maybe we can find a way to slip a blunder into Honk's prompter," somebody said.

"Don't you even *think* about doing that," Ann said. "First of all, Kate would fire you if you tried, and second of all, getting caught at it could throw the election to Honk, and then you'd have to go to a place where I could never find you."

"I have an aunt in darkest Mexico," the prankster responded.

"Do yourself a favor, and leave now."

The woman raised both hands. "Just kidding."

"Stop kidding and get to work. We've got to make these last days the smoothest and most credible of the campaign," Ann said. "Keep it high-minded and keep it straight: no missteps, no pranks, and thus, no backfires. And above all, *not a single leak to the press about this poll!* Everybody clear on that? If this leaks, I'll find out who did it and personally kill that person!"

There was a murmur in the room, and the group began to disperse.

"Good, now let's get to work." Her cell phone rang, and she recognized Stone's number, stepped into her office, closed the door behind her, and drew the shades, signaling to the staff that she wished to be left alone. "Hi," she said, trying to sound cheerful.

"You sound as though you're trying to sound cheerful," Stone said. "And you aren't making it."

"Oh, God," Ann said, her voice quavering, "I've got the most awful feeling we're going to lose this thing, and I can't tell anyone but you."

"What's gone wrong?"

"Nothing has gone wrong, that's what worries me."

"You're worried about nothing going wrong?"

"Not exactly. We just got a new private poll, a big one that cost us a lot of money, and we're trailing Honk among independent likely voters by eight points, with only two percent undecided, and we can't figure out why. Kate has been brilliant, but for some reason, the very people we're counting on are drifting away from her. Don't breathe a word of this to anybody!"

"Certainly not. This sounds like a bad poll to me. They must have made some sort of mistake in the sampling, or something."

"From your lips to God's ear," Ann said. "Tell me some good news."

"I bought a house in Paris."

"That *is* good news! I'll have somewhere to hide from the world next week!"

"You're not going to need a hideout, but if you did, you'd like this one. It has a little mews all to itself, in the seventh arrondissement, just off the Boulevard Saint-Germain. It's walled off from the world, but Paris is just outside the gates."

"It sounds heavenly. Can I come right now? I won't even pack, I'll just go straight to the airport and disappear forever."

"No, you won't, you'll go to work as if that poll didn't exist, and you'll win it."

"When are you coming home?"

"The grand opening gala is later this week. I'm getting on the Strategic Services jet immediately afterward and heading straight for Washington. Kate has offered me the Lincoln Bedroom for election night."

"I know about that, I'll be there, too, but down the hall."

"Then you can sneak in and sleep with me in Abe's bed."

"I'd sleep with you in anybody's bed."

"I'll count on that."

"I've gotta run. I have three thousand things to do."

"Then go do them. I'll see you soon."

STONE HUNG UP and sighed. That poll sounded like very bad news for Kate.

"You ready for dinner?"

"Yes!" he called back.

"Upstairs or downstairs?"

"I'll meet you in the study!" He got into a robe and trotted down the stairs, fear for Kate replacing hunger in the pit of his stomach.

S tone bounded out of bed, shaved, showered, dressed, and bounded down the stairs, ready for breakfast.

"You slept well," Holly said, dishing up eggs and bacon.

"You exhausted me," Stone said.

"That's a good reason." She kissed the top of his head. "I've gotta run—a meeting about you at the station."

"I'm flattered, but I don't believe it for a moment."

"Believe it—there's already an office pool on whether you'll make it as far as the grand opening of l'Arrington."

"How are you betting?"

"I haven't decided yet—maybe after the meeting." She kissed him, grabbed her coat, and headed for the door. "Oh, by the way," she called over her shoulder, "the pistol Rick loaned you is in your sock drawer."

"Thanks!"

Stone finished his breakfast alone, then went into the living room, his sense of well-being evaporating. He picked up a book and tried to read; no use. He played some Jerome Kern on the piano; no effect. Cabin fever began to set in.

He got up and paced a bit, then, seeking fresh air, he opened the front door and stepped out into the mews. His guards were, apparently, on the boulevard side of the big doors. He walked carefully around the cobblestoned area in front of the house, then inspected the flowers growing in the center turn-around but quickly ran out of walking space. He heard the phone ring inside the house and ran back indoors to answer it, but when he picked it up, the caller had already hung up.

He collapsed into one of his new/old armchairs and wondered what to do next. Then there was a tapping on the window behind him. He looked around to see one of his guards peering inside.

"Good morning," the man said when he opened his door. "There's a man who shouldn't know where you are, asking to see you, and he has a woman with him." He handed Stone a card that read "Yves Carrier, Woodman & Weld."

"It's okay, you can let him in," Stone said. "He's from the Paris office of my law firm."

"Right you are," the man replied. He went to the big doors, opened the small inset door, and waved in a man and a woman. The man was young and fashionably dressed; the woman was middle-aged and motherly-looking.

Stone ushered them into the house and offered them chairs.

"I've brought some documents for your signature, with regard to the purchase of . . . this house, I presume?"

"You presume correctly, M'sieur Carrier."

"Please call me Yves," he said. "Madame Roche has come along to attest to your identity and signature. Is your passport handy?"

"I'll get it." Stone went upstairs and rummaged through his things until he found the passport. He also found the gun in his sock drawer and dropped it into his pocket, not that he thought Monsieur Carrier and Madame Roche represented a threat. He ran down the stairs and handed the passport to the woman, then took a seat.

She looked at him, then at the passport, then did it again. *"D'accord,"* she said.

Carrier began handing Stone documents; he signed them and handed them to Madame Roche, who stamped and signed them. Stone tried to read one, but it was in French.

"I must say," Carrier said, looking around, "that you have got yourself a very good buy here. Properties of this sort in this neighborhood are going at much higher prices than you are paying."

"I'm delighted to hear it," Stone said, signing the last of the stack of documents and handing it to Madame Roche. "I love a bargain."

"And this is a very beautiful room," Carrier said.

"You should have seen it the day before yesterday," Stone said.

"Pardon?"

"I've done a bit of redecorating."

"Ah."

"Is there anything else I need to do?" Stone asked.

"No, we'll e-mail these to Mr. Cabot right away for his signature. Assuming he signs, the house is yours. And there's a car, too?"

"Yes, in the garage, but I haven't bothered to look at it yet."

"Let's go and check it for a registration," Carrier said. He followed Stone to the garage, and they approached the lump under a tarp in one of the two bays. Stone pulled the cover away to reveal a Mercedes four-door sedan of the late seventies or early eighties. Except for some dust, it looked almost new. A pair of wires ran from under the hood to a receptacle in the garage wall: a battery charger, apparently.

He opened the driver's door and inspected the creamy leather, which was in excellent condition. He sat down, found the key in the ignition, and turned it. The car started instantly. He switched it off quickly, not wishing to be found dead of asphyxiation.

"Do you see a registration anywhere?"

Stone rummaged in an envelope and handed Carrier some papers.

Carrier inspected them, then went to the rear of the car and had a look at the license plate. He came back and handed Stone the documents. "It's registered to a name at the American Embassy," he said, "and it has diplomatic tags. Park anywhere you like."

"I like the sound of that," Stone said, pocketing the keys and following Carrier back inside the house.

"Well, I hope you'll be very happy here," Carrier said. Hands were shaken, and he and his notary left.

Stone found himself again alone with himself. Curious, now, he went through the kitchen into the garage and, using his house key, let himself into the staff flat. It was a small but comfortably furnished suite with bedroom, bath, and kitchenette. He went back into the house and took the elevator to the top floor, where he inspected two en suite bedrooms with a common sitting room between them. One floor down, he found a large bedroom with a sofa and two chairs in front of the fireplace, much like the master. He walked downstairs, found his book again, and sat down beside the fire. He had been there for only a moment when he heard two loud pops from the direction of the boulevard. That brought him to attention, but after a moment he dismissed the noise as a vehicle backfiring and went back to his book.

Before long he rested his head against the chair and dozed off.

51

Stone was dreaming of Election Day in the United States. He was in a large hall with a movie-theater-sized television screen, and Kate Lee was making a gracious, very affecting concession speech. "In the end," she was saying, "it was all the fault of someone named Stone Barrington, who I had never heard of until last week. . . ."

Stone tried to speak, but someone put tape over his mouth and something black over his eyes, and his hands were taped to the arms of his chair.

"There," a man's voice said. "He will be most comfortable."

Stone, still half in his dream, tried to protest that Kate's loss was not his fault, but he stopped himself. This part with the tape and the blindfold and the chair was no dream. He reoriented to the extent that he could. First, he wondered if he had been drugged, but he decided that was impossible, since the only thing he had eaten or drunk since yesterday had been given to him by Holly.

"*Mmmph!*" he said, wanting to speak.

"Just rest quietly, my friend," a soothing voice said, in an accent that was not British or American but was otherwise not immediately identifiable. "He will be here soon, and then you will know everything."

Stone was not looking forward to knowing everything, beyond the point where he had been so rudely awakened. He wondered if Holly really had drugged him, and if this event were part of what had been discussed at her meeting at the Paris station. He was still drowsy, and gradually he nodded off again, surprised at how relaxed he was.

He was awakened by a woman's voice, speaking in French, apparently coming from another room. There was protest in her words, whatever they were.

Then someone untied the blindfold, and Stone blinked in the unaccustomed light. A man stood in front of him; he had a very good look at a silver belt buckle before the tape was ripped from his face. "Shit!" he said.

"Sorry, Mr. Barrington, it was the most humane method," the belt buckle said. Then the man backed away from him and sat down in the chair opposite Stone's. He slowly recognized Jacques Chance, prefect of Paris police, brother of Mirabelle.

"Thank you for your humanity," Stone said.

"Jacques!" the woman in the next room said insistently.

"Silence, *ma chère*," Jacques replied. "We will be done here soon."

"Done with what?" Stone asked, honestly curious.

"That remains to be seen, Mr. Barrington. If you are co-operative, you will autograph some papers for me, and then I will be gone, and you will still be alive."

Stone didn't like what he imagined as the alternative. "Let me guess," he said: "You want me to sign over my interests in the Arrington hotels?"

"Quite right," Jacques replied. "But you will be handsomely compensated. I have in my possession a banker's check for thirty million euros, with your name on it. I should think that would be a very happy alternative to what the Russian gentle-man would have me subject you to, should you fail to sign."

"I suppose this is what you would call the carrot or the stick," Stone said.

"Be happy it is not the frying pan or the fire," Jacques said. "It could easily have been so, were it not for Mirabelle's per-suasions."

"*Merci beaucoup*, Mirabelle!" Stone called out, so that she could hear him in the kitchen.

"Sign the papers, dummy!" she called back.

"All right," Stone said, "I'll sign the papers. If you will be kind enough to untape me."

"Of course," Jacques said, rising and coming toward him with a pocketknife. "I should mention that there are two strong and dangerous men standing behind you, who would take it amiss if you did not behave properly."

"I will be the soul of propriety," Stone said.

Jacques cut through the tape holding both wrists, and Stone removed what remained and tossed it into the fireplace. He turned his head to see another man sitting at the desk with a stack of papers before him. "Here, please," he said, indicating the chair next to him.

Stone got up, walked across the living room, and sat down at the desk. The man uncapped a Mont Blanc pen and handed it to him, then he riffled through a few pages of the stack. "Here," he said, pointing to a blank space. Stone signed. "Here," the man said at another page. Stone signed. This continued until Stone had signed a dozen times, then the man extracted an envelope from his inside coat pocket, produced a check, made out as Jacques had indicated, and a sheet of paper, where he indicated Stone was to sign once more. Stone signed.

The man returned the check to the envelope and handed it to Stone. "You may deposit it into your account at any bank in the world," he said. He picked up the stack of papers, put it into his briefcase, and snapped it shut. He retrieved his pen, capped it, and placed it in an inside pocket. "My business is concluded here," he said to no one in particular. "I bid you good day." He left by the front door.

"Mr. Barrington," Jacques said, "I wish to thank you for being compliant in these circumstances. It would have been unpleasant for me to watch someone of whom my sister is fond be subjected to great harm and, very likely, a painful death. Now my business is also concluded here, and I, too, wish you a good day."

Jacques went into the kitchen and came back holding Mirabelle's hand.

"I am so sorry for all of this, Stone," Mirabelle said, then she was whisked out of the house by her brother. She came back a moment later. "I want you to know that these stupid rumors about Jacques and me are ridiculous lies!"

"I never doubted it for a moment."

She left again.

Stone got out his cell phone and called Marcel duBois. He was connected immediately.

"Hello, Stone."

"Marcel," Stone said, "I have just been compelled, under duress, to sign away my ownership in the Arrington hotels. Or at least, I think that's what I signed—it was in French."

"I'm sorry to hear that, Stone, as I have just done the same thing, and under duress, as well."

"Are you safe now?"

"I believe so."

"Then call your attorney, explain things to him, and have him take every legal action to stop the sale. And don't cash the check."

"Stone," Marcel said, "I don't know if that is the right thing to do."

"Marcel, right or wrong, it is the *only* thing to do."

"They have made very serious threats."

"Ignore them. I'll call Mike Freeman and have you removed to a safe place at once."

Marcel sighed. "All right, Stone, if you insist," Marcel replied. "But I am very much afraid that you and I are out of the hotel business."

"We'll see about that," Stone said.

52

Stone called Yves Carrier at the Paris Woodman &
Weld office and explained what had happened.
"I should tell you that I signed the papers 'Steve
Ballington.'"

Carrier laughed loudly. "Nevertheless, I will take immediate steps to stop any transfer of title to the company in every
country in Europe. You should have the New York office stop
transfer in the United States. Someone might not notice the
discrepancy in the signatures."

Stone hung up and called Bill Eggers, the managing partner in New York, and brought him up to date.

"I can't imagine how they think they can get away with
that," Eggers said. "Whatever you do, don't cash the check."

"Right," Stone said. He hung up and called Mike Freeman and asked him to reinforce Marcel's security. "That's twice they've gotten to Marcel," he said. "You've got to move him."

"I don't have a safe house at my disposal," Freeman said.

"Then bring him to me here," Stone said. "There's plenty of room. We'll need more security, though. Jacques Chance has already gotten into the house."

"I'll send people at once. What's the address?"

Stone gave it to him, then hung up the phone. He called Rick LaRose and told him what had happened.

"I don't understand how Chance got past my people," Rick said. "Hang on while I call them."

Stone hung on impatiently.

Rick came back on the line. "No answer. Something's wrong."

"No kidding? What happened to the men who were supposed to be on the roof?"

"They weren't due there for another hour."

"Mike Freeman is sending people. See that yours don't shoot his." He hung up, then Holly called.

"Rick told me what happened. It's partly my fault."

"Which part?"

"I put a sleeping pill in your orange juice at breakfast. I was concerned about you, and I thought more sleep would help."

"Thank you for your concern—the pill worked all too well."

"I'll be there as soon as possible," she said. "Hang on a minute." She covered the phone and spoke to someone. "Our two men on the gate were taken out with a dart gun. They're still unconscious in a car outside your gate."

"Great."

"Rick has replacements on the way."

"Mike Freeman is sending people, too. He's having Marcel brought here. I'll put him in one of the upstairs rooms."

"Just hang on until everybody gets there. Be ready to shoot anybody who won't identify himself properly."

"I hope I can get out of this without killing somebody," Stone said. "That could keep me in France for weeks, while it's being investigated."

"I hope that doesn't happen, but it's preferable to having you killed."

"I'll go along with that," Stone said. He hung up and pulled his chair near the window and peeked past the curtain, so he could see into the mews, the pistol Rick had given him in his hand.

HOLLY ARRIVED half an hour later with reinforcements and oversaw the placement of her people. "They're on the roof here and across the street. There are two men just inside the gates, and they'll all be replaced in shifts."

Mike Freeman arrived with Marcel duBois in tow, carrying a small suitcase, and Stone took him upstairs in the elevator and got him settled in, then he went back downstairs. Lance Cabot was seated before the fireplace.

"How the hell did you get to Paris so fast, Lance?"

"I never left," Lance replied.

"So when I called you, you were in Paris?"

"My phone works everywhere, Stone."

"Of course it does."

"I've just come from a meeting with Prefect Chance."

"Jacques?"

"His father, Michel. He is extremely embarrassed about the conduct of his son. He says he has not been able to find him or speak to him since the newspaper revelations of his selling out to the Russians. He is determined to see Jacques in prison."

"The old man is not going to be of much use to you, is he? In the circumstances?"

"I hope I talked him out of resigning. We need someone we know in that office, until this business is resolved. The good news is, because of the revelations about Jacques in the papers, Yevgeny Majorov is now a fugitive in France. Michel has put his best people on the search for him."

"What about Jacques? Is he a fugitive, too?"

"Yes, but not officially. Michel just wants him detained before he hurts someone. He was shocked at the news of Jacques's visit with you today."

"Not as shocked as I was," Stone said.

"Well," Mike said, "it seems that we have a virtual army on our side now. I hope the French police can prevent Majorov from leaving the country."

"That's more than my people can do," Lance said. "We're now in a situation where we have to rely on the French. I had hoped to avoid that."

"I don't want to avoid it," Stone said. "I want Majorov and Jacques in custody."

Marcel came into the room. "I was thinking, perhaps we should issue a statement to the press about what has happened—perhaps even hold a press conference."

Lance shook his head. "It's not a good idea for Stone's name to appear in the press," he said.

"I don't mind, if it will help find Majorov," Stone replied.

"You're forgetting our election at home," Lance said. "Your name has already been linked to Kate's in the press once, she doesn't need that happening again at this late date."

"Of course, you're right," Stone said. "I guess I'm not thinking very clearly."

"All you can do now, Stone, is just hunker down here until Majorov pops up somewhere, and the French can lay hands on him."

Stone knew he was right, but he didn't like it.

Stone woke with a jerk; he had been dreaming, but he couldn't remember what, except that it was very important. He tried to go back to sleep to regain his dream, but an image popped into his head that kept him awake. It was something he had seen back in Los Angeles, at his son Peter's hangar at Santa Monica Airport.

Stone sat up in bed. The image was of a Gulfstream jet, the one that Yuri Majorov, Yevgeny's brother, had later died in. There was something unusual about it, something that made it different from other Gulfstreams, but he couldn't get it straight in his mind. It was a symbol something like the old USSR crossed hammer and sickle, but not quite; something was different about it. He swung his feet onto the floor and sat on the edge of the bed, trying to re-create the scene in his mind. He was standing by the open hangar door when the Gulfstream taxied past him, headed for the terminal building. The symbol was painted on the engine nacelle, so it was directly in his line of sight as the airplane passed him. It was in red paint. What was more, he had seen it somewhere recently.

"What's wrong?" Holly asked from the other side of the bed.

"I just remembered something," Stone replied. "Lance said that his people couldn't prevent Majorov from leaving the country."

"That's right, there aren't enough of our personnel in Paris to cover the airports and the train stations."

"If Majorov wants to leave the country, he won't go by train—he'll fly in his own jet."

"There are an awful lot of those," Holly said, "and I happen to possess the useless knowledge that there are fourteen airports in and around Paris."

"He'll be leaving on a Gulfstream 450."

"There are a lot of those, too, and we don't have a tail number. And they all seem to have a similar paint job."

"Not this one," Stone said. "It has a sort of takeoff on the Soviet hammer and sickle on the engine nacelle, but instead of a sickle crossed by a hammer, it's a sickle crossed by a Kalashnikov assault rifle. I saw it at Santa Monica Airport, and again at Le Bourget when we arrived here. I had forgotten about it."

Holly sat up. "We've got to call the Paris police," she said.

"Bad idea," Stone replied. "First of all, why would they listen to us? We're Americans, and we can't explain ourselves in French."

"Lance can call Michel Chance, the prefect. His jurisdiction is the Île-de-France, which includes all fourteen airports."

"He won't be leaving from thirteen of those—he'll be leaving from Le Bourget, where Charles Lindbergh landed after his flight across the Atlantic."

"Why do you think that?"

"Because when Charles de Gaulle Airport opened, Le Bourget became the airport of choice for corporate jets like the Gulfstreams. I just told you, I saw the Majorov jet when we landed there."

"That's right, we did. Let's wake up Lance."

"I've got a better idea—wake up Rick LaRose and tell him we'll meet him at Le Bourget."

"It's a big airport, where are we going to look for the airplane?"

"At Landmark Aviation, where we landed. It was being hangared there."

"Lance will kill me if I don't wake him up," Holly said.

"All right, get dressed and wake him. And when you call Rick, remember to tell him we're leaving here for Le Bourget and to let his people outside the house know not to fire on us."

"I'll certainly remember that," Holly said, getting into some jeans.

LANCE CAME downstairs dressed, but unshaven. "All right, Stone, tell me about this."

"Didn't Holly tell you?"

"You tell me."

"I saw the airplane, first in Santa Monica, then I saw it at Le Bourget when we arrived on Mike Freeman's Gulfstream. I just couldn't remember where I had seen it before—now I do."

Lance produced a cell phone and pressed a number. "Rick? We're on. Stone says for us all to meet at Le Bourget, at Landmark Aviation." He listened for a moment, then hung up. "All right," he said, "let's get going."

Lance had, apparently, been on the phone before, because there was a Mercedes armored van waiting for them in the mews.

"How far is it to Le Bourget?" Holly asked.

"Seven miles," Lance replied. "It seems like a lot farther in traffic, but there's no traffic this time of the day. Driver, step on it—use the flashing lights if you have to, but no siren."

Stone was pressed into his seat by the acceleration.

54

They didn't bother with the Périphérique; they went straight north, through the heart of Paris. It astonished Stone how little traffic they saw along the way.

"Director," the man in the front passenger seat called, "where at Le Bourget?"

Lance gave him directions to a security gate near Landmark Aviation. "Rick LaRose will meet us there."

Ten minutes later they drew up at a security gate bearing a large sign in several languages, to the effect that admittance was available only to those with the proper credentials. At their appearance, the gate slid open, beeping loudly. Just inside, next to a small guardhouse, Rick stood waiting for them with half a dozen other men.

Lance slid open a door. "Rick, I assume you have the proper credentials for us to be admitted."

"I do," Rick replied. "A two-hundred-euro note satisfied that requirement." He produced a map of the airport and a small flashlight. "Here's Landmark," he said, then pointed at a lighted ramp a quarter of a mile away. "There are several large hangars. I've sent some men to reconnoiter. They'll call us." He held up a small handheld radio.

"How long do we have to wait?" Lance said.

"Until they call us. The airplane could be in any of the Landmark hangars, or it could have already departed. That seems unlikely, however. We checked with the tower, and no flight plan for a Gulfstream jet has been filed since sundown yesterday."

"Check with the tower again," Lance said.

Rick produced a cell phone, dialed a number, and, in excellent French, conducted a brief conversation, then hung up. "A Gulfstream 450 has filed for Saint Petersburg"—he consulted his watch—"departure in thirty-five minutes."

"Can you see it on the Landmark ramp?" Lance asked.

Rick got a pair of binoculars and trained them on the FBO. As he did, a voice was heard from his radio. He listened. "That's our guy," he said. "An FBO employee tells him a Gulfstream is being pre-flighted by three pilots, a stewardess, and a maintenance crew in Hangar Two." He pointed. "The doors are closed."

"Tell your guy," Lance said, "to find a way to observe—*only observe*—the interior of the hangar. I want to know if there are any passengers in the hangar or on the airplane, and I want to know if any vehicles bearing such persons arrive at the hangar."

Rick transmitted the orders. "He'll get back to us. Do you want us to go over there now?"

"Not until we know what we're getting into," Lance said. "I don't want a firefight on French soil." He turned around. "Stone, you're a pilot—what's the best way to temporarily disable a jet airplane without causing a fire or an explosion or much of a fuss?"

"Fire a round into the nosewheel," Stone said. "It would take at least an hour, perhaps much longer, to replace it, even if they have a tire readily available."

"An hour to change a tire?"

"It's not a car," Stone said, "it's an airplane, and the mechanics who work on it have to follow strict procedures in the maintenance manual. It's time-consuming."

"Would the pilots start the engines in the hangar?"

"No, the thrust from those two big engines would likely blow out the back of the hangar. They'll tow it onto the ramp with a tractor, and they'll start the engines there."

Lance turned back to Rick. "If or when any attempt is made to tow the airplane from the hangar, tell your guy to shoot out the nosewheel tire, employing stealth, preferably with a silenced weapon. He should not fire at any person, even if fired upon."

Rick transmitted the order. "Tell me when you want me to go," he said to Lance.

"I want to know if any passengers are on that aircraft before I make any decisions."

"My guy is working on it."

Lance sat very still and waited, his eyes closed. Stone thought he might be napping.

Presently, Rick's radio squawked, and he put an ear to it. Then he leaned into the van. "Two large vans just arrived at a door on the other side of the hangar. Six men and two women went inside, and their luggage is being taken into the hangar, as we speak."

"Tell your guy to do his work on the nosewheel, then report back."

A minute passed, and the radio squawked. "The tire is out," Rick said.

"Right," Lance said. "How many men do you have at your disposal?"

"Eleven," Rick replied, "not including you, Stone, and Holly."

"That should be enough. Let's get over there, and I want your men to cover the large doors at the front and any other egress. No one is to leave the hangar—should anyone try, shoot to wound, not kill. Go!"

"Now, driver," Lance said, "give their vehicles a two-minute head start, then drive over to the hangar they are covering and park this van to the right of the main door, where there's a smaller door in the big door."

"Yes, sir," the man said.

They all sat and waited for two minutes, by Stone's watch. "Lance," he said, "what is your plan?"

"Plan?" Lance asked, as if surprised. "I plan to be reasonable, if I can."

"And if you can't?"

"Then all hell will break loose," Lance said. "Time to go," he called to the driver.

The van began to move toward the hangar.

As the armored van rolled across the tarmac toward the hangar, the huge doors began to rise and fold, and from the left, a tow tractor appeared from the darkness and moved toward the big jet.

The van pulled up to the position Lance had ordered. They had a very good view of the front of the Gulfstream, to just past the main door. Lance produced an iPhone, tapped the Contacts icon, then tapped in a name. "Ah," he said, then tapped the resulting phone number. He put the instrument to an ear and listened for several rings, then he apparently got an answer. "Yevgeny!" he said, smiling, as if the man were an old friend. "It's Lance Cabot here. Good morning! Yes, I know it's rather early, but I wanted to speak to you before you abandoned Paris." He listened. "On your way, are you? Well, not quite. If you will be kind enough to send someone to inspect your nosewheel, you'll find that it's in no condition to roll, and thus, neither is that beautiful Gulfstream of yours. Go ahead, I'll wait." He held the phone a few inches from his ear, and shouting in Russian could be heard. The door of the airplane swung down, and a uniformed pilot ran down the air stair and to the nosewheel, which was quite flat. He ran back up the stairs into the aircraft.

"Had a look, have you?" Lance said into the phone. "Did your pilot explain to you that, with a deflated tire, your airplane cannot move? Good, now let's have a little chat. I'm sitting outside your hangar in an armored personnel carrier"—he winked at Stone—"and the prefect of the Paris National Police is here along with, I don't know, perhaps fifty of his men, all suited up for combat, armed with automatic weapons and raring to go. He's asked me to speak to you, since you, your family, and I are, well, old acquaintances, sort of. Prefect Michel Chance would like for you, your traveling companions, and your airplane's crew to walk down your air stair into the hangar, and he would very much appreciate it if none of you were holding a weapon or anything else in his hand." He held the phone away from his ear, and Stone could hear more shouting in Russian. "Now, now, Yevgeny, we don't want that beautiful airplane of yours all shot full of holes, and the hangar burning down with the airplane inside it and you and your friends inside the airplane—do we? Of course we don't, but I'm very much afraid that that is exactly what will happen if all of you are not down the stairs in, say, sixty seconds. Let me make it easy—I'll count down for you: sixty, fifty-nine, fifty-eight . . ." Lance continued to count.

Stone turned to Holly. "What do we do if Lance gets to zero?"

"Duck," Holly said.

"Fifteen, fourteen, thirteen—running out of time, Yevgeny! Twelve, eleven, ten, nine—hurry up, now, trigger fingers are getting itchy! Eight, seven, six, five, four"—the count slowed—"three, two and a half, two, one and a half, one . . ."

A woman's hand was stuck out the door, waving a handkerchief.

"Come along, now, Yevgeny, nobody's going to shoot a woman waving a lace handkerchief. Let's get them all out."

One by one, people appeared and walked down the airstair, the men with their hands in the air. Finally, Yevgeny Majorov came out the door and followed them to the shiny white concrete floor of the hangar.

Rick's men spilled into the hangar, weapons at the ready, and began securing the group's hands with plastic ties.

Lance was making another phone call. "Prefect Chance, please," he said. "I apologize for the hour. Just tell him it's Lance Cabot on an urgent matter." He covered the phone. "I think he must be asleep," he said. "His wife sounded very grouchy." He smiled. "Good morning, Michel. I'm terribly sorry to call at such an ungodly hour, but I have some very good news for you that just won't wait for the sun to come up. I'm out at Le Bourget, and some of my people and I have detained Yevgeny Majorov, just as he was about to fly off to Saint Petersburg. You see? I told you it was good news, didn't I? Well, I suppose we could deliver them all—there are about a dozen, including some air crew—to a police station of your choice, but I thought for appearance's sake that you might want to run out here with a contingent of France's finest and take them into custody. After all, we're guests in your country, and we don't want to presume upon your hospitality. Good, Michel. We'll look forward to seeing you and your people in an hour or so. *Au revoir.*" Lance hung up. "Ah," he said, "that was very satisfying."

"It was satisfying to me, too," Stone said.

Rick LaRose walked up, smiling. "All accounted for," he said.

"Good, good," Lance replied. "Prefect Chance and his merry men will be here fairly soon. In the meantime, why don't you turn their pockets out and then have a look in their luggage. You never know what you might find."

Rick turned to his work.

Lance put his hands on Stone's and Holly's shoulders. "Now, since we have a few minutes on our hands, why don't I have a chat with Comrade Majorov?"

Stone said to Lance, "Mind if I sit in on your conversation?"

"Ordinarily, I wouldn't mind," Lance said, "but I think Mr. Majorov is likely to be more forthcoming if it's just the two of us." He strode over to Majorov, took him by the arm, and marched him up the airstair into the Gulfstream.

"Well," Holly said, "that was almost exciting."

"Don't complain—nobody got hurt," Stone said. They stood around for a few minutes watching Rick's men go through the passengers' pockets and luggage, and apparently not finding anything worth their attention.

Then a white truck rolled into the hangar. Two men in

white coveralls got out and produced a tire, a toolbox, and a tank of compressed nitrogen.

"That was fast," Stone said. "I once had to replace a tire and it took half a day."

"Gulfstreams get better service than Mustangs, I suppose," Holly replied.

The two mechanics went to work changing the tire. They jacked up the front of the airplane, removed the wheel, removed the tire from the wheel, then worked the new tire onto the rim. That done, they inflated it with nitrogen, bolted it onto the airplane, and departed in their truck.

"Wow," Stone said.

Lance appeared in the doorway of the airplane and beckoned to Rick, who ran up the stairs and conferred with his boss. For a moment, he seemed to disagree with Lance, but Lance seemed to speak firmly to him, and he backed down. He started back down the stairs, but Lance stopped him with a word. Rick took something small from a pocket, handed it to Lance, then continued down the stairs. He had a few words with his men, and they began, rather haphazardly, repacking the passenger luggage, then reloading it, under the direction of one of the pilots.

Then, to Stone's astonishment, Rick's men began cutting the plastic ties from the passengers' wrists, and they all reboarded the aircraft.

Lance reappeared without Majorov, came down the stairs and had a word with the pilot, who got on his phone, then handed Rick his pocketknife. Lance came over to Stone and Holly. "Let's get out of here," he said, and waved to the van's driver, who drove into the hangar.

The FBO's tow tractor reappeared, hooked up to the aircraft, and began rolling it out of the hangar. Someone inside the airplane retracted the airstair and locked the door.

"Lance, what's going on?" Stone asked.

"Into the van, both of you, if you please."

Stone and Holly climbed into the van. When Stone took a breath to protest, Holly squeezed his knee and shook her head.

From outside came the sounds of jet engines spooling up; lights at the Gulfstream's wingtips began to flash, and a red beacon at the top of the tail began to rotate. The airplane began to move toward a taxiway.

"Lance," Stone said, "where are Michel Chance and his gendarmes?"

"Asleep in their beds, I should think," Lance replied.

The van stopped on a taxiway for a moment, then, with a very loud roar, the Gulfstream rolled past them down the runway and left the ground.

Stone was angry. "What the hell just happened?"

"What just happened," Lance replied, "was that a solution to a very sticky problem was negotiated to the satisfaction of nearly everyone involved."

Stone was flabbergasted.

"I think, Stone, that you and your business partners will not be hearing from or dealing with Yevgeny Majorov or his friends again, and they will make no attempt to enforce the agreement you signed. Oh, by the way, may I have that banker's check for thirty million dollars that Jacques Chance gave you?"

Stone produced the check from an inside pocket and handed it to Lance, who deposited it in his own inside pocket. "There," Lance said, making a dusting motion with his hands, "all done." He smiled a little smile. "And we won't be discussing these events again. With anyone, not even each other. A matter of national security, don't you see?" Then he closed his eyes, sat back in his comfortable seat, and took another of his little naps.

STONE AND HOLLY were deposited back in the mews as the sun began to rise. There were no guards present at the gates or on the roof.

They went upstairs, undressed, and climbed back into bed.

"Can you tell me what happened out at Le Bourget?" Stone asked her.

"I should think it's obvious," Holly said. "Apparently, an accommodation was reached with Comrade Majorov."

"That doesn't make any sense. Why would Lance want an accommodation with Majorov?"

"Apparently, because it's in Lance's interest to do so. Apparently, it's in your interest, too, since Majorov, apparently, won't try to kill you anymore."

"And no gendarmes showed up, so that wasn't a real call that Lance made to Michel Chance?"

"Apparently not," she replied.

"Why do you keep saying 'apparently'?"

"Because all this is only speculation on my part," Holly said. "But it makes sense, if Majorov is an asset of Lance's—part-time, of course. Yevgeny does have a business to run. The good news is, he appears to be out of the hotel business."

"If all Lance had to do to fix this was to call Majorov, why didn't he call him a long time ago, instead of waiting until Majorov was trying to leave the country?"

"Apparently, because tonight he had leverage he didn't have before. Majorov was desperate to leave the country, Lance had prevented that and he thought the gendarmes were on the way."

"This is all too complicated for me."

"That's because your mind is not devious enough for intelligence work."

"Is that a bad thing?"

"No, sweetheart." She leaned over and gently bit a nipple, and Stone's thoughts of Majorov were replaced by other thoughts.

57

S tone was having a sandwich in the mews house the
next day, while Holly attended yet another meeting at the CIA station, when his phone rang.

"Hello?"

"It's Ann."

"I thought you were submerged in work, never to surface
again."

"Actually, that's a pretty good description of what has happened to me over the past couple of weeks. When are you coming home?"

"Tomorrow night is the grand opening of l'Arrington, and
we're going from that directly to the airport, so I'll be home
early the following morning. I'll take a day to rest, then, on

Election Day I'll borrow a Mustang from Strategic Services and fly down to Washington. Can I give you a lift?"

"What time of day?"

"What time of day would you prefer?"

"Five-ish?"

"As long as the 'ish' doesn't run too late. I believe we're both expected for dinner at the White House family quarters—that, and a lot of TV, until we know the result."

"Okay, pick me up at four sharp. I'll have a car meet us at, where, Manassas?"

"Right. Given the traffic, I should think we'll be there by seven."

"Perfect."

"How are things going?"

"We've been slightly ahead inside the margin of error on most polls. A couple have shown Honk creeping up, but I'm ignoring those."

"So, you're in a horse race, then?"

"I wish we weren't, but we are. I keep expecting something explosive from Honk's campaign, but it hasn't happened yet, and if he's going to pull something, he's running out of time."

"I hope there's no chance of my name coming up again."

"So do I. It was after the paternity rumors that the polls started getting tight. Your name will not pass my lips until the polls have closed on the West Coast, maybe Hawaii."

"That's just fine with me," Stone said. "I hate getting phone calls from reporters."

"You seem to have charmed the last one you talked to," Ann said.

"Wasn't I supposed to?"

"Well, yes, but I'm jealous anyway. Since the apology by and disappearance of Howard Axelrod, she's been slyly complimentary about you to a couple of people I know, and the news reports following Axelrod's exit from the scene have been good to you. Even the evening news shows have gone out of their way to point out that you and Kate were defamed, and Rush Limbaugh expressed regret that he didn't have you to kick around anymore."

"I'm glad I wasn't around to hear all this," Stone said. "It would have made me nervous."

"What have you been doing with your time the last few days?"

"Oh, consulting with Marcel duBois on the grand opening, kibitzing with our board on last-minute details, that sort of thing."

"No grand meals at expensive restaurants?"

"Nope, I'm lunching on a ham sandwich as we speak."

"No company of gorgeous women?"

"Of course, every chance I get!"

"I knew that—you didn't have to tell me. After all, I set you free, didn't I?"

"Caged no more!"

She laughed. There was a noise from her end like a door opening, people talking, then the door closing again. "Hang on a minute, will you?"

"Sure." Stone took another bite of his sandwich and tried to listen to the muffled conversation at the other end, which went on for three or four minutes.

"I'm back," she said, "and this is not going to make you happy."

"What isn't going to make me happy?"

"A reporter just came in here and said he'd heard a rumor out of the CIA—that means he's got a source inside—that the Agency has spent a lot of money protecting you from those Russians that hate you so much while you've been in Paris."

"My goodness, am I supposed to be that important?"

"According to his source, Lance Cabot thinks you are."

"I think I can say, without fear of contradiction, that any report of anything positive Lance Cabot has ever said about me would be grossly overblown and should be dismissed out of hand."

"But you are a consultant to them, aren't you?"

"I had a cousin, now deceased, who was a rival of Lance's at the Agency, so I've had dealings there at widely separated intervals."

"Nothing you can talk about, I suppose."

"I wouldn't talk about it, even if I could. The inconsequential nature of the me/Agency relationship would be an embarrassment. I'd rather people thought it was more important."

"So I don't have to worry about anything coming out of Honk's campaign about you and Lance Cabot?"

"They can always make up something, I guess. I can't stop them."

"I pointed out to the reporter who was just in here that sullying your name backfired on them last time—resulting in the resignation of a high campaign official. I think he'll print that."

"Okay by me."

"I gotta run. Call me when you're back in New York and over your Gulfstream lag."

"Will do." They both hung up. Stone had been feeling relaxed, but now he was nervous again.

58

Stone called Lance and got a voice mail beep. "Trouble at home," Stone said. "Call me soonest." He hung up and finished his sandwich, then the phone rang.

"Lance?"

"Dino."

"Sorry about that, pal. I had a call in to him."

"Where the hell have you been? You've checked out of the suite, and your cell phone hasn't been working."

"I'm sorry about that—it got wet, and I had to get it replaced."

"Are you okay? The Russians haven't kidnapped you?"

"I'm reliably informed that the Russians are no longer a threat."

"Oh? Are they all dead?"

"I'll tell you more when I see you. Are you done with your conference?"

"A couple of days ago. We stayed over to see some sights and get the free ride home after the big do."

"Why don't the two of you come to dinner tonight?"

"Come to dinner where?"

"Oh, I didn't tell you—I bought a house."

"You're insane."

"You won't think so when you see it." Stone gave him the address. "Seven-thirty?"

"Okay. Then I want to be brought up to date."

"I'll tell you everything." They hung up, and Stone called Holly, got the beep. "I've invited Dino and Viv to dinner tonight at seven-thirty. Stop by Fauchon again and pick up something delicious for four, okay? If you can't do it, let me know and I'll pick it up." He hung up.

TWO HOURS passed before Lance returned his call. "All right, Stone, who's after you now?"

"Not I—Kate. Someone in your bailiwick has leaked to a reporter that you're spending outrageous money on protecting my ass."

A brief silence. "Any idea who?"

"Of course not—you should have a better idea than I."

"Any idea which side of the Atlantic we're talking about?"

"Nope, but how would anyone on the other side know what's going on over here?"

"It would have to be someone highly placed," Lance said.

"Ann Keaton said she got it from a reporter who got it from a source inside the Agency."

"That is disturbing."

"The reporter is treating it with caution, but the election is Tuesday. This would not be a good time for you to have to deny it."

"Deny it? I don't deny things, except before a congressional committee."

"There are Republicans on congressional committees," Stone said. "In fact Henry Carson is on the Senate Intelligence Committee."

"You have a point. Let me see what I can learn." Lance hung up without further ado.

Stone washed the dishes from breakfast and went in search of a book in his new library. He settled on an old biography of Huey Long, but he had trouble concentrating.

HOLLY BUSTLED into the house bearing four shopping bags and a wine carton slung over one shoulder. "Good thing I got your message," she said. "We would have starved."

"Have you talked to Lance today?"

"Yes, this morning, but he suddenly got busy after lunch and has been cloistered for the rest of the day."

Stone told her his news.

"Well," she said, "this could hardly have come at a worse time."

"No kidding."

"Lance badly wants Kate elected," she said.

"I didn't know he was sentimental about politics."

"He's sentimental about his job. He wants to keep it when the next administration comes in, and he's not real close to Carson."

"I feel helpless," Stone said.

"You'll have to rely on Lance."

"Now I *really* feel helpless."

"Did he express any ideas?"

"Not really."

"Lance is at his best when he's in personal jeopardy. He'll come through."

"Time is short."

Holly looked at her watch. "You're right. Dino and Viv will be here in twenty minutes, and I have to make it look as though I prepared all this food." She ran for the kitchen while Stone tidied the living room.

Dino and Viv were on time.

59

Dino walked into the house and looked around the living room. "Holy shit!" he said. "How the hell did you find this?"

"You might say Lance found it for me, though he didn't mean to."

Dino accepted a scotch and Viv a martini. "Explain."

"It was a CIA safe house, belonged to a former station chief here, and the Agency bought it."

"And you bought it from the Agency?"

"From an Agency foundation, the same one that I bought my cousin Dick Stone's house from. I think I've discovered that the foundation would rather have cash than real estate. My local attorney says it's a bargain."

"What's upstairs?" Viv asked.

"A master suite and three bedrooms. There's a garage and a staff flat on the other side."

"I'll buy the staff flat from you," Dino said.

"Think of the place as your own, whenever you want it."

Holly came in with hors d'oeuvres.

Viv bit into one. "This is delicious," she said.

"Oh, it's just a little something I whipped up," Holly replied.

"The hell you say."

"All right, everything's from Fauchon."

"What's Fauchon?"

"A kind of heavenly grocery store that sells the groceries already cooked."

"I like the sound of that," Viv said.

"Okay, enough about groceries," Dino said. "I want to know what's been going on. Why were you in a safe house, Stone?"

Stone took a deep breath and gave Dino and Viv an account of his time.

"Well," Dino said, when he had finished, "you've been having a lot more fun than I have. Has Jacques Chance been arrested?"

"As far as I know, no."

"The guy's a nutcase," Dino said. "Somebody ought to throw a net over him."

"I look forward to that happening," Stone said.

"I've had a couple of long conversations with his old man, Michel."

"What's he like?"

"He's a stiff, but he's a smart one. Very old-school, but a cop all the way through."

"Did he say anything about his son?"

"I was present when somebody brought up the subject. He just turned and walked away. Like I say, very old-school. Rumor around the conference was that Jacques is being searched for, but quietly. Apparently, removing the prefect of Paris police is complicated."

They finished their drinks and moved to the dining table at one end of the room, where Holly had distributed Fauchon's finest.

Stone tasted and poured the wine, and they sat down to dinner. Stone's phone rang. "Hello?"

"It's Lance."

"Hang on." He excused himself and took the phone into the study. "Okay," he said.

"Your little insight turned out to be correct," Lance said.

"What insight was that?"

"The Senate Select Committee on Intelligence—a staffer who had formerly worked in Carson's office."

"How did you deal with that?"

"Had a chat with Henry Carson, who denied all knowledge, said the woman was acting out of her own enthusiasm for his candidacy, nothing to do with his campaign."

"Do you buy that?"

"No, it's not necessary to buy it. He said all that before I had a chance to brief him. He mentioned the woman's name."

"Funny how he already knew about it."

"I thought so, too. I had a chat with the reporter in question. He's willing to hold the story."

"What did you have to give him?"

"An interview—or at least the promise of one—after the first of the year. I don't give many interviews, so it will be something of a coup for him."

"Thank you, Lance."

"You're quite welcome." Lance hung up.

Stone returned to the table. "It looks as though Lance has the story contained."

"Where was the leak?" Holly asked.

"A staffer on the SSCI, used to work for Carson."

"Whew!"

"Will she get fired?" Dino asked.

"I didn't ask."

"If Carson wins, I'll bet she turns up on the White House staff."

"Let's don't talk about 'if Carson wins,'" Stone said. "I shudder at the thought."

The following morning, Stone and Holly packed their clothes and moved back into the suite at l'Arrington; it seemed a good idea, since they were departing from the hotel for the airport. Stone sent his tails to be pressed and his shoes to be polished, while Holly unboxed her new gown from Ralph Lauren and hung it in her dressing room.

While she was fussing with that, Stone's phone rang.

"Hello?"

"It's Ann."

"Hi, there. How are you?"

"Relieved."

Oh, no, he thought. "Relieved, as in fired?"

"No, silly—relieved as in relieved. Less anxious, if you like."

"Have you changed your meds?"

"No. I mean, I'm not on meds. Except sometimes, when I need to sleep."

"Why are you less anxious?"

"Because the reporter I told you about yesterday told me he wasn't filing the story. He said he didn't have backup sources."

"That's good news, isn't it?"

"It certainly is. What I want to know is, how did you do it?"

"Do what?"

"Get the story killed."

"Ann, I don't even know the reporter, never met him. I don't know his editor or his publisher, either."

"Then how did you do it?"

"Why are you assuming I did something?"

"Because you're the only person I told about the story."

"You didn't tell Kate or Sam Meriwether?" Meriwether was the holder of Will Lee's old Senate seat and Kate's campaign chairman.

"No."

"Why not?"

"Because I had a feeling you were going to fix it."

"You overestimate me."

"I thought you would deny it, but I warn you, when you get home I'm going to torture you until I get the whole story."

"I'll look forward to that."

She laughed. "Anyway, I'm relieved, and I wanted you to be relieved, too."

"I'm relieved."

"Have a good time at your gala tonight."

"That will be torture, too." They said goodbye and hung up.

That evening, when Stone came out of his dressing room, Dino was standing at the bar in the living room, sipping scotch and dressed in white tie and tails.

"I don't know how you ever got me to have this suit made," Dino said.

"I told you you'd need it, eventually."

"You're usually right about these things."

Viv walked in from next door wearing a champagne-colored sequined dress and a piece of jewelry around her neck that Stone figured had cost Dino three months' pay.

"Wow," he said.

"Me, too," Dino echoed. "Everything was worth every cent of what it cost, and I don't want to know what that was."

"That is the highest compliment you've ever paid me," Viv said, kissing him lightly, so as not to smear her lipstick.

Holly made her entrance, her auburn hair piled on top of her head, in her strapless emerald green gown that set off her hair and skin color. Everyone oohed and aahed, and they had a drink while waiting for the other guests to arrive.

Stone opened the terrace doors and they stood, watching the elegant crowd as they spilled out of big black cars—

Bentleys, Rollses, Mercedeses—and passed slowly through the doors and the security checkpoint, where metal detectors and X-ray machines were set up. Well-dressed guards from Strategic Services—no uniforms—greeted them while armored weapons specialists patrolled the courtyard and the rooftops.

"Everything seems in good order," Stone said. When the bulk of the crowd had passed in, the women made one last pass at the living room mirror, adjustments were made, and they all took the elevator down to the main floor.

A string orchestra was playing light classical music in the big lobby, and handsomely uniformed waiters passed among the glittering crowd with trays of champagne and canapés. The American ambassador to France arrived through the main doors, accompanied by Lance Cabot. Stone took Holly's hand and drew her closer. "Help," he whispered.

"Don't worry, I'll fight her off," Holly replied.

Just behind the ambassador, Marcel duBois entered alone to applause and made a beeline for Stone. They shook hands and embraced.

"Is it going well, do you think?" Marcel asked.

"It's going beautifully," Stone said.

Marcel shook everyone's hand and admired the women. "You didn't cash the big check, did you?" he asked Stone.

"Lance Cabot took it from me before I could," Stone said.

Then a momentary hush caused everyone to look toward the entrance. Mirabelle Chance was seen first, in a flame-red gown, no doubt of her own creation, then behind her appeared her brother, Jacques, resplendent in a dress uniform with much gold braid. The crowd began to chat again, no doubt about the infamous Chances.

"He must have designed that uniform himself," Holly said. "Shades of General Custer!" Everybody laughed but Stone.

"I didn't think he'd have the gall to show up," he said. "Perhaps I should go and greet him properly." He started to move.

"Don't," Holly said, taking his arm and tugging to stop him.

"He's probably in better shape than you are," Dino said.

Marcel spoke up. "Perhaps pistols at dawn!" That relieved the tension, and they turned their attention to meeting and greeting the other guests.

Lance and the ambassador wandered over, and Stone took shelter behind Holly. "What's the news from the States?" Lance asked Stone.

"I've heard that the reporter didn't file his story, because of a lack of corroboration. There is much relief in the Kate campaign."

Lance leaned in. "I let it be known to Henry Carson that if the story did emerge, there would be consequences," he said quietly, "in the form of a story tracing the leak to his campaign."

"Very good," Stone said.

Then chimes were rung, and the crowd filed into the grand ballroom and found their tables and seats, while a jazz trio played the American Songbook.

"Take a look at that," Dino said, holding up a beautiful steak knife from his place setting.

"They were especially made for our hotels by an American custom knife maker," Marcel said. "A set of them will be party favors for each of the gentlemen guests, while the ladies will receive a specially created perfume called 'Arrington.'"

Dino chuckled. "After all that security at the door, the guests have been armed, and these things are razor sharp. I hope no fights break out."

Soup and fish courses were served, then thick slices of boeuf à la Wellington, for which the knives were intended, came next, and the accompanying wines were superb.

After dessert, Peter Duchin, who had been flown in from New York, led a big band for dancing.

Jacques Chance and his sister swept around the floor, and people made room for them. No one was smiling, Stone noticed.

He noticed something else, too: at the edges of the room uniformed French gendarmes were appearing in twos and threes.

Jacques Chance noticed, too, and he maneuvered Mirabelle toward the bandstand, where an American singer was performing.

From his angle of view, Stone noticed something else: cradled in Jacques's hand was the haft of one of the hotel's steak knives, its blade concealed in his sleeve.

Stone began to move quickly toward the couple, but he knew he wasn't going to make it in time.

S tone felt as if he were moving in treacle, dodging waiters carrying cheese and glasses of port. He struggled on.

Jacques Chance, clutching his sister's wrist, dragged her toward the bandstand, where he shoved the singer out of the way and stood before the microphone. *"Attention!"* he shouted. The orchestra and the crowd began to fall silent.

Stone grabbed a cane from the back of the chair of an elderly gentleman and continued moving toward Jacques, knowing that he was about to witness a murder/suicide.

Then a tall, rigidly erect, white-haired man in a police uniform appeared at the edge of the dance floor and shouted, "Jacques Chance!"

Jacques had raised the knife in his hand but was momentarily transfixed by the sight of his father in this unlikely setting, and he hesitated, giving Stone his chance. He hooked Jacques's hand with the cane and jerked him off the bandstand. The knife skittered a few feet away, and Jacques fell to one knee, still clutching Mirabelle's wrist and taking her with him.

With Jacques disarmed and momentarily off balance, Stone took a wide swing with the cane and connected with the side of Jacques's head, creating a resounding *whack* in the silent room. Jacques shook off the blow; he let go of Mirabelle and began making his way across the floor toward the knife, finally reaching out for it. His father walked up to him and stamped heavily on his son's wrist, breaking it with a loud *snap*. The elder Chance turned toward Stone and said, *"Merci, M'sieur,"* then the area before the grandstand was swamped by gendarmes and Jacques disappeared in their midst.

Stone was roughly pushed back by a policeman, and he took the opportunity to make his way back to the table, rehanging the cane on the back of its owner's chair along the way. He sat down next to Holly and mopped his face with his napkin. Pandemonium reigned at the bandstand. Peter Duchin got up from the piano, shouted something to the orchestra, and gave them a downbeat. "La Marseillaise" filled the ballroom, and even the policemen stood at attention.

"Good work," Holly said.

Dino spoke up. "The cane was a nice idea."

"Let's get out of here," Stone said. He took Holly's hand and led the others toward a side door. By the time the anthem had ended, they had escaped to the elevator.

THEY LANDED at dawn, just after Teterboro opened for business. The sleepy passengers disembarked, said their goodbyes, and their luggage was transported to the front of the terminal, where their drivers took their luggage and Stone's man, Fred Flicker, awaited with the Bentley. He and Holly piled in.

"Home," Stone said wearily.

"My home first," Holly said, "to leave my bags with the doorman. I'm back in the real world now, and I have to go to work."

"So be it," Stone said.

STONE LEFT his luggage to Fred and let himself into his house. His secretary, Joan, who lived in the house next door, was up early to greet him.

"Welcome home," she said. "Do you want to see the mail and messages?"

"I want my bed," Stone said, kissing her on the forehead, and, getting into the elevator, "I'm going to sleep all day, if I can. Hold off the world."

He fell into bed naked, alone, and exhausted.

———

THE FOLLOWING DAY, Tuesday, Election Day, Stone voted at his neighborhood polling station, which, he noted, was packed, then collected Ann at her apartment building. Fred drove them to Teterboro, where the borrowed Strategic Services Citation Mustang awaited them on the ramp.

"I've never flown into Washington in a private jet," Ann said, settling into the cockpit right seat.

"It's more fun than the airlines," Stone said, starting an engine.

They landed at Manassas, Virginia, and a waiting car drove them to the White House. A butler and a Secret Service agent rode with them in the elevator up to the family quarters, and their luggage was made to disappear.

Kate Lee left a group by the fireplace and came to meet them. Hugs and kisses were exchanged, and drinks appeared. Stone knew, perhaps, half of the two dozen people in the room. Two large flat-screen television sets had been set up, and there was a buffet table.

"I'm so happy you could join us," President Will Lee said, shaking Stone's hand and kissing Ann. "It's going to be an exciting evening. I guess we're going to find out if we have to move out of here."

"Either way, you've both had a great run," Stone said. "I hope to see it extended."

"Well, if it is extended, we'll be all lined up for a series of firsts: first female president, first pregnant female president, first child born to a president, first born in the White House, and so on."

"And first former president not to move out at the end of his term," Stone pointed out.

Stone and Ann finished their drinks, got plates of food and glasses of wine, and settled into a sofa to watch the next president of the United States be elected.

AUTHOR'S NOTE

I am happy to hear from readers, but you should know that if you write to me in care of my publisher, three to six months will pass before I receive your letter, and when it finally arrives it will be one among many, and I will not be able to reply.

However, if you have access to the Internet, you may visit my website at www.stuartwoods.com, where there is a button for sending me e-mail. So far, I have been able to reply to all my e-mail, and I will continue to try to do so.

If you send me an e-mail and do not receive a reply, it is probably because you are among an alarming number of people who have entered their e-mail address incorrectly in their mail software. I have many of my replies returned as undeliverable.

Remember: e-mail, reply; snail mail, no reply.

When you e-mail, please do not send attachments, as I never open these. They can take twenty minutes to download, and they often contain viruses.

Please do not place me on your mailing lists for funny stories, prayers, political causes, charitable fund-raising, petitions, or sentimental claptrap. I get enough of that from people I already know. Generally speaking, when I get e-mail addressed to a large number of people, I immediately delete it without reading it.

Please do not send me your ideas for a book, as I have a policy of writing only what I myself invent. If you send me story ideas, I will immediately delete them without reading them. If you have a good idea for a book, write it yourself, but I will not be able to advise you on how to get it published. Buy a copy of *Writer's Market* at any bookstore; that will tell you how.

Anyone with a request concerning events or appearances may e-mail it to me or send it to: Publicity Department, Penguin Group (USA) LLC, 375 Hudson Street, New York, NY 10014.

Those ambitious folk who wish to buy film, dramatic, or television rights to my books should contact Matthew Snyder, Creative Artists Agency, 9830 Wilshire Boulevard, Beverly Hills, CA 98212-1825.

Those who wish to make offers for rights of a literary nature should contact Anne Sibbald, Janklow & Nesbit, 445 Park Avenue, New York, NY 10022. (Note: This is not an invitation for you to send her your manuscript or to solicit her to be your agent.)

If you want to know if I will be signing books in your city, please visit my website, www.stuartwoods.com, where the tour schedule will be published a month or so in advance. If you wish me to do a book signing in your locality, ask your favorite bookseller to contact his Penguin representative or the Penguin publicity department with the request.

If you find typographical or editorial errors in my book and feel an irresistible urge to tell someone, please write to Sara Minnich at Penguin's address above. Do not e-mail your discoveries to me, as I will already have learned about them from others.

A list of my published works appears in the front of this book and on my website. All the novels are still in print in paperback and can be found at or ordered from any bookstore. If you wish to obtain hardcover copies of earlier novels or of the two nonfiction books, a good used-book store or one of the online bookstores can help you find them. Otherwise, you will have to go to a great many garage sales.